DEFENDER

THE ENHANCED, BOOK NINE

T.C. EDGE

TABLE OF CONTENTS

CHAPTER ONE

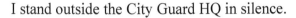

I stand outside the City Guard HQ in silence.

The constant hum of activity, created by the clearing of the wreckage of the High Tower, and the relentless footfall of both soldiers and civilians, has temporarily gone mute. A thousand people stand, unmoving, unspeaking, their eyes set on a single sole. Waiting for her to speak.

The sun is still rising, and the air is cool and calm. The perpetual cloud of dust that grew in the wake of the High Tower's fall has begun to fade away. Slowly but surely, the centre of the city, the centre of Inner Haven, is beginning to be restored.

The people are a collage, brought here from all walks of life. Surviving Savants, now serving a new master. City Guards doing the same. Rebels of the Nameless, rugged and worn. Enhanced and Unenhanced alike, gathered from all corners of the city, now standing as one in the face of a greater threat.

All now fall under the same banner. The banner of freedom.

Yet beyond the city, within the REEF, Artemis Cromwell still lurks with his sycophants and Stalkers. And over in the eastern quarter, the Con-

Cops still control the food production plants and factories, awaiting their master's orders.

They remain, to me, our enemy. But not at this time. Right now, we have no choice but to stand side by side and face the incoming threat head on. Because it is coming, and there's no hiding from it here.

The people have yet to discover the truth of what's going on. To them, the ceasefire in place speaks of our victory. They think that a longer, more permanent peace is currently being negotiated. They think that this city has seen the last of its fighting.

They're wrong.

Just beyond the City Guard HQ, a small stage has been erected. It was hastily constructed in the early hours of the morning, not long after Zander and I returned from the outerlands with confirmation of the threat we're facing. Now, that threat needs to be spread to the people. They deserve to know the truth.

The cameras have been set in place, ready to beam my grandmother's face across all the working screens in the city. All residents across Inner Haven, and those still in Outer Haven, will be waking to the announcement that they are far from safe. That the city that has seen so much suffering will now be set against a new foe, one that we still know so little about.

I watch my grandmother now as she steps up onto the podium. The last few days have seen her go without much sleep, and the stress is taking its toll.

It's visible through the expression on her face, the deepening wrinkles and growing pallor of her skin. And her movements too, creaking and aching with every step as she climbs towards the microphone.

She's not alone in that. Dark circles now adopt a permanent position below so many sets of eyes. A haunted, fearful expression appears to have taken hold on so many faces. Few of us now sleep as much as we should, as our bodies need. We catch what rest we can, when we can, and continue to run on fumes. It's become something I've quickly grown used to through necessity alone.

The silence in the crowd deepens as Lady Orlando moves ahead of the microphone. It's a stark image to see her here, under the yellow morning light, with the carcass of the High Tower painting a terrible backdrop. Its ghosts still haunt me, and yet they're drowned out by so many others. Others I've killed. *So many lives I've now taken…*

They will come at me in my nightmares for as long as I live. I know that now. I know that full well. Yet here, awake, I can keep them at bay. Thrust them into the recesses of my subconscious, just waiting to creep back to the light when I fade off into my dreams.

I do so now, dismissing them all as Lady Orlando surveys the crowd. And in that crowd are so many I care for, so many who remain under threat. Brenda and Tess stand close, already aware of the incoming threat. I see their weary eyes and know they've been struggling to sleep as well. Yet they adopt weak smiles too, expressions they have to constantly hold in order to keep the kids calm.

Drum is with them, having spent his first night back from the mines in Compton's Hall. He'll now be assigned to a new post within the military, drafted into some patrol or set in position against the border wall in Outer Haven. His countenance is firm, eyes solid. He, too, will be quite aware of what we're facing.

Others at the heart of the Nameless dot the areas closest to the stage. Beckett, Freya, Rycard. I spot Sophie too, not with her husband but away in the crowd, their duties keeping them apart. And right by my side, my brother and Adryan stand, the former with his left arm bandaged from the battle with the Bear-Skins; the latter so close I can feel his warmth in the early morning cool.

We all stand, along with a thousand others, and not a single word is spoken as Lady Orlando opens her mouth, and begins.

"Good morning, everyone," she says, her voice floating calmly across the throng. "I have gathered you here to set you straight. Over the last couple of days, a great deal of rumour has been circulating regarding the ceasefire in this city, and the current state of peace. Some of you have heard that a new attack is coming, and that Director Cromwell is preparing to retaliate for our capture of Inner Haven. That isn't true. In fact, quite the opposite…"

Her words bring a rumble of confusion and whispers. She quietens them with her next words.

"As of right now," she continues, "the extremities

of Outer Haven are being bolstered and fortified. We have hundreds of our soldiers on patrol and watching the perimeter, and the City Guards who remain under Director Cromwell's command are aiding us in this task.

"We are, ladies and gentlemen, currently working together in the face of a common threat. Only last night, we got confirmation from two of our trusted soldiers that a large force is coming from the west. Right now, we have little further information to go on, and are currently liaising with Director Cromwell to further our understanding of this potential threat."

Her words bring a further round of murmurs. These are more vocal, the idea of working with Cromwell clearly rather repellent to several members of the crowd.

"I understand your concerns," calls out my grandmother. "Director Cromwell remains a threat to us, and we are not going to fall into the trap of trusting him completely. However, the simple fact is that, should this incoming force turn out to be hostile, we may need to combine our forces into order to repel them.

"Many of you here right now have only recently returned from the mines. For those who aren't aware, and for all the tens of thousands of you listening across the city, know that it was Director Cromwell's Stalkers who escorted our people back to safety. I have heard accounts from several people telling of how the Stalkers protected them. They did this under Artemis' command, and we can take that

9

as some sign of cooperation should we need to fight alongside them."

More grumbles spread from the throng. Several people shout out their aversion to the idea. Again, my grandmother cools them with graceful lift of her hand.

"We have little more to tell you now," she goes on. "We will be doing all we can to learn as much as possible about this threat, and if we're called to fight, we will. Hopefully, it won't come to that. I will always choose a course of negotiation over war if one is possible, but if such a thing turns out to be impossible, we will work with Director Cromwell to deal with the threat.

"Here, in Inner Haven, you will remain safe. It is highly doubtful that any army will be able to breach our walls…"

The crowd find their voices again. I hear several queries being shouted from their midst.

"How large is this army?"

"When will they get here?"

"Are they Enhanced? Are they hybrids?"

Lady Orlando deals with them as best she can.

"We don't yet know the exact size of the force or their make-up. Estimates suggest at least five thousand. They are crossing the plains west of here, and will most likely reach the western woods within a few days…"

"A few days!"

"Five thousand!"

The crowd begin to rumble more ferociously. I wonder quite why she's being so honest, given her supreme ability at keeping secrets. I like the transparency, though. We're all in this together, after all.

As the calls get more wild, however, Beckett storms up onto stage, his voice like a force of nature as he bellows across the plaza.

"Quiet yourselves down!" he shouts. "We have everything in hand, and there's no reason for you to worry. As Lady Orlando says, you're perfectly safe here. No number of wildmen can breach our walls, and our soldiers will keep you safe. If, and that remains a big *if*," he growls, "we need to operate alongside Cromwell's Stalkers, then we will…"

"And what about after?" shouts a man. "What will you do with Cromwell after? Make peace? Go back to war with him?"

The crowd get on board and start murmuring the same query. Beckett looks to Lady Orlando, who retakes the mic.

"We will deal with that when we come to it. Right now we must maintain our focus on this force from the west. Please, continue with your lives and duties, and know that we're doing all we can to prevent further war from escalating."

She steps away and off the stage before anyone else can disrupt her. More calls begin to flow from the crowd, building up as she's quickly escorted back into the City Guard HQ by her protective guard. I stand and listen to the tumult for a moment, before following closely behind along with the other high profile members of the Nameless.

Alongside me, Adryan hurries.

"You think that was a good idea?" I ask him. "Telling them all what's going on?"

He shrugs.

"I suppose they deserve to know, though it was always going to lead to more questions, given the fact that we have so little information."

"Yep. Well hopefully we'll find out a bit more ourselves soon enough. You believe that she'll go to negotiate with these people?"

"Of course. Negotiation is always the first port of call in these sorts of situations. If they're coming to exact some sort of revenge on Cromwell's treatment of them, then it's best to show them that he's no longer in control around here."

"Personally, I'm not sure they'll care about who's in charge. Their slight is with the 'big city with all the lights'. Maybe I've grown embittered by all this, but I'm thinking they're coming here to destroy the city, not try to occupy it. I mean, they're from the wilds, Adryan. They don't want to live here. They just want to destroy us."

I find Adryan looking at me with a curious expression as I speak.

"Embittered," he says, nodding. "Though, that's completely understandable. And for what it's worth,

I reckon you're right. But, regardless, Lady Orlando will still wish to commune with these people as early as possible and see if she can strike a bargain."

"Well, how about this for a bargain – we hand them Cromwell and let them do whatever they want to him," I growl. "Throw in his Stalkers for good measure. Then maybe they'll leave us alone."

I finish with a huff, knowing none of that will happen.

"Sounds reasonable to me," smiles Adryan. "Easier said than done, but highly appealing."

"Yeah, just the problem of the Stalkers primed to kill us all if anything happens to their damn director. Much as I hate him, I've gotta hand it to him on that one. Unless we can take out the Stalkers, or lure them into some sort of trap, old Artemis is pretty much untouchable."

Adryan nods silently, and through into the City Guard HQ we go.

We gather in the main forum, where Lady Orlando addresses the prime members of the Nameless towards the rear. The only absentee is Commander Burns, who remains under guard in the infirmary.

Last night, having returned from the outerlands, Zander headed down there to have his shoulder seen to, and to perform another brief inspection of Burns' mind in a hunt for hidden orders. He came up with nothing. Only by Burns' personal recommendation has he remained down there with two guards outside the door.

Still, I know that's a temporary measure, and his wisdom will be important in the days to come.

"OK, are we all set?" asks my grandmother, surveying the small gathering.

She doesn't wait for anyone to offer a vocal answer.

"Excellent," she continues. "Now let's go ahead and find out just what Artemis has to say."

Typical of the times, the morning rushes on without allowing us time to breathe. Together with Zander, Adryan, Beckett, Rycard, and Freya, and along with a large cohort of hybrids including Marker, we begin moving through the rear of the building towards our convoy at the back.

Our sights are set once again on the western gate of Outer Haven. And, once again, it's time to meet with my grandfather.

CHAPTER TWO

The meeting with Cromwell occurs in the same place as it did before.

This time, however, we don't step beyond the western gate of Outer Haven, but stay within the city limits as we await our guest. With our soldiers once more posted in position atop the walls and inside the gate, we quickly hear warning from above that he approaches.

As before, he comes with his band of Stalkers for protection, several dozen of them by his side and taking position outside the gates. Only he, however, is permitted entry past. And this time, he comes with only a single ally.

No other members of the Consortium join him, and only Agent Woolf appears by his side. They enter through the gate, grinding open under the late morning sun, the gathering of black-clad Stalkers loitering behind.

Our own party await him, and a question immediately rises on my grandmother's lips.

"Just you this time it is, Artemis?" she asks, barely acknowledging Woolf's presence.

I suppose the agent isn't here to negotiate, but

merely to use her considerable mental gifts to ensure that no lies are being spoken on our side of the discussion. Those eyes of hers are always watching, and those lips are always smirking. I pray for the day when the expression is permanently wiped from her face.

"Yes indeed, Cornelia. The other members of the Consortium have their hands full right now."

"I see. Well, given how all they ever do is echo your words they're unlikely to be missed," crackles Lady Orlando. "Now come, let's get out of the sun."

We move into the small control building, set to the side of the gate, and the two leaders take position at the central table within the recreation room. The rest of us hover about, Adryan the only addition, and the members of the Consortium the only absentees, from the previous meet.

Immediately, Cromwell is quick to pick Adryan out.

"Ah, Mr Shaw," he says. "I see you've made it this time. How are you?"

"I'm quite all right, Director Cromwell," answers Adryan stiffly. "Eager to press on."

"Ah, aren't we all. We have little time for small talk. Is that what you're getting at?"

"You are correct, Director. I am merely here to observe. I would rather not speak with you to be perfectly honest unless I have something important to contribute."

Adryan's eyes show a measure of distaste for the

man that most Savants would have a great deal of trouble displaying. Cromwell, meanwhile, merely nods and hunts the rest of us with his eyes, that devious little smile of his always hovering on his lips.

"Adryan's right, Artemis," says Lady Orlando. "Now, as I informed you on the radio, Brie and Zander have confirmed this force you told us of. Our estimates show at least five thousand. They're heading eastwards across the plains and will be at the western woods within a few days. I assume this isn't news to you."

"By no means, Cornelia. I know more than you do on this matter, I can assure you. It is, however, nice to see that you're on board and have quickly performed your own checks. Regrettably, though, I'd say your estimations are rather on the short side. We believe the numbers could be twice that."

Several sets of worried eyes dart at each other around the room before settling again on Cromwell.

"And how do you come to this conclusion?" asks Lady Orlando.

"As I told you before, we were monitoring foreign threats from the High Tower for many years before you saw it to the ground. A gathering of ten thousand strong wasn't something we considered unlikely. I hope you realise that this necessitates the need for our cooperation?"

My grandmother doesn't answer immediately. I feel a sinking feeling in the pit of my stomach once again at the prospect of teaming up with the man.

Something just feels so off about it, and I'm all too aware that everyone else shares the assessment.

Still, there appears to be no other option.

"We will form a temporary pact, Artemis," confirms Lady Orlando after a brief silence. "Our preference will be to send out a negotiation party to meet with the leaders of this force and see exactly what they want. As you well know, the city's defences are being fortified, though we obviously have no time to reinforce the entire perimeter. We will require you to inform the City Guards still loyal to your cause to aid us. Many still remain within Outer Haven, and we need all hands on deck just in case this potential enemy should choose to attack…"

"Oh, they *will* choose to attack," says Cromwell. "I will send orders to my men, as you say, but make no mistake, Cornelia, sending a negotiation party to meet with this army will be folly. They are here to destroy the city and nothing less."

"And you know this how?"

"For goodness safe, Cornelia, will you listen to what I've been saying? I have told you several times now that we have been monitoring this threat. People have come to the city for years, and we have read their minds and discovered where they've travelled from. We know full well that beyond our borders, we have enemies who harbour a desire to destroy us and nothing else. They don't see this city as a shining light as we do. It is a blight to them, and they wish it gone…"

"They wish revenge," I find myself cutting in. "It's your fault they're coming here. They're coming here because of the way *you* treat people. And good riddance if they have their way with you."

I stare at my grandfather with a hatred that runs deep. He merely seems amused at my outburst, a quizzical look flashing across his face.

"Ah, I see you still have that fire in your eyes, Brie," he says to me. "Perhaps you're right. But regardless as to your opinion on the matter, they're coming here to kill us all." He turns back to his former wife. "Negotiating with them will not be possible, Cornelia. I do wish you'd trust me on this."

"Well, unfortunately I am in agreement with Brie here," she says, turning to me with a smile. "We don't trust you, Artemis, and we will look to negotiate first and foremost."

Cromwell considers it for a while, and seems to realise that there's nothing he can do to change her mind.

"OK," he says. "So tell me, who will you be sending exactly? Surely you won't be heading into the wilds yourself?"

Lady Orlando shakes her head.

"No, I will not. Beckett will take the lead along with several of our more potent soldiers. We will fly the banners of peace and treat with these people."

Cromwell's eyes swerve towards Beckett, standing typically tall and stiff.

"Good luck, Mr Beckett," he says coolly. "I fear you won't be returning to the city should you set out there to 'talk' with these people."

"That sounds like a threat," growls Beckett.

"Not a threat, no," retorts Cromwell. "Merely a statement of likely fact." He looks back to Lady Orlando. "Might a make a suggestion, Cornelia – if you are keen on treating with these people, might I suggest you send out soldiers you're willing to sacrifice. I am well aware that Mr Beckett here is a highly capable hybrid and military commander. It would be foolish to send him to his death."

"I won't be going to my death, Director Cromwell," seethes Beckett. "I'm going to talk and nothing more."

"Yes, perhaps *you* are. But don't expect them to talk back. They will kill you if they get a chance along with whomever you take along for the ride. So I reiterate my point – don't waste any of your more powerful soldiers on this. They will be needed when this army attacks in full. And believe me – they will."

His words seem to have some impact, a veil of doubt settling over the room. For a few moments I share looks with my allies and see the ripple of concern flash through their minds.

Even Lady Orlando seems to be giving the advice a little more time to process in her mind.

"I have more information that might help you make your decision," Cromwell continues, taking his opportunity to break the short silence. "I have deployed some of my scouts to the far reaches of the western woods and beyond. I have some incredibly gifted Hawks among my Stalkers, and they have been relaying information back to me regarding the movement of this incoming force. I told you, I know more than you on this matter. And unfortunately, you are wrong when you say they'll take several days to get here…"

"Speak plainly, Artemis. You're saying they'll be here sooner?"

"Oh, not all of them, no. The force is splitting. The main army is travelling at the rate you suggest, and will arrive, as you say, within days. However, a forward force of Dashers and hybrids appear to be making speedier progress. It appears to be a unit designed to clear the way through the woods for the rest when they arrive. So, as I say, if you send Mr Beckett and some of your soldiers ahead, they will likely be going to their deaths."

"You underestimate me, Director," growls Beckett. "I have no fear of these wildmen. If I can deal with your Stalkers, I'm sure the same is true of these barbarians."

"Ah, perhaps you're right. But once more, Mr Beckett, you don't really know what you're talking about, do you? There are people out there unlike any you've ever faced. I find it ironic for you to suggest I don't underestimate you, and yet you're doing the very same thing to the very people who are coming here to destroy you."

"OK, Artemis," says Lady Orlando. "How many are we talking here? This forward unit?"

"Hard to know for certain. At least a hundred or two, and perhaps more. They will spread through the western woods and clear them out, killing anyone they come into contact with. That is their aim…"

"What about Rhoth," I breathe, my worries bubbling to the surface. "His whole tribe is down there. They'll all be killed."

Zander nods, adding his voice to the debate.

"He's a stubborn man," he says. "I advised him to head eastwards, and even offered the Fangs sanctuary in the city. He declined. They'll either kill them all, or recruit Rhoth into their army. Neither is particularly palatable."

"Well then, there appears to be only one way to combat this," says Cromwell, his voice beginning to bristle with an energy that makes me nervous. "We ambush them on their path. I will allocate some of my strongest Stalkers, and you can do the same with your hybrids. If we can destabilise this forward force, it will severely weaken their advance."

"Sounds a little too convenient for you," says Beckett, staring daggers at the man. "You just advised us to keep our stronger hybrids back, and now you're telling us to send them all out there to fight? You don't have a secret agenda, do you, Director Cromwell?" The sarcasm in his voice is impossible to miss.

"I stand by what I said," confirms Cromwell immediately. "Sending a few men would have meant your deaths, yes. Sending a larger force, along with my Stalkers, will not. It is a standard battle tactic and will hold them back and give you more time to sure up the city's defences…"

I see Lady Orlando turn to Rycard and Freya, standing together to one side. I know that both are coordinating in seeing to the buttressing of the walls and gates.

"That is true," says Rycard. "We could do with some extra time."

"Freya?" asks Lady Orlando.

"I agree," booms the white-haired woman's deep voice. "The more time we have, the better."

"No, no, that's not good enough," says Beckett. "I smell a rat here. The Director is manipulating us, as usual. He wishes to get us all out there away from the city and kill us himself. He'll set that task to his Stalkers, I guarantee it."

"Utter nonsense," says Cromwell, waving his hand dismissively. "How exactly would killing you aid me? You know full well what's coming. I'm certain my Stalkers would do their best, but not even they may be able to hold back this storm alone. Do not be so naïve to think that there are not extremely powerful hybrids out there, Mr Beckett. There are. And they're coming."

I look at Beckett, who continues to adopt the position of 'doubter-in-chief' when it comes to anything my Machiavellian grandfather says. Yet his concerns are generally based off of distrust for the man, rather than logic. Looking at the latter, he might just be right.

And, after Kira's disappearance, we're all well aware of the sorts of people lingering out there in the distant lands. I saw it myself, and I saw it in West's memories too. And clearly, if these people are sending soldiers ahead, then they're quite confident in what they can do.

"We are aware of the sorts of threats we might be facing," confirms Lady Orlando calmly. "However, we are all very much in agreement with Beckett in so far as trusting you goes, Artemis. You have a solid track record of manipulating people and so you'll understand Beckett's concerns."

Cromwell concedes on that point, nodding and holding up a conciliatory hand.

"Fair enough. Yes, you are entitled to doubt me, of course. Most likely, you probably believe that I'm going to try to use this situation to my benefit?"

He looks around the room. All but Beckett just stare. The gruff commander, however, nods quite firmly.

"I see that I'm right," Cromwell says, offering a smile. "Now, how can I show you that I have no ulterior motive here? All I wish is to defeat this incoming force and maintain peace within the city. I am well aware that your victory in Inner Haven has altered the status quo. My plans have been put to bed on that account. Now, should we combine our forces to defeat this army, we can then discuss a possible future that can be mutually beneficial."

Beckett huffs audibly.

Cromwell ignores him and goes on.

"So," he continues, "we stand here at an impasse. I have laid it all on the line. I have nothing to hide, I can assure you."

"Prove it," comes a rather loud voice from the back. All eyes turn to Freya, white eyebrows hovering low. "Let Zander look inside your head. If you're telling the truth, he'll find out."

The gaze of the room shifts to my brother.

"I could try," he says, nodding. "If Director Cromwell will allow it?"

Cromwell lifts an artificial smile.

"I welcome it, I truly do," he says brightly. "Perhaps you'll then see that I have no wish here but to defend the city and its people."

As he speaks, a memory flashes in my mind. During my first meeting with the man, up at the summit of the High Tower, I'd tried to creep into his thoughts and found myself immediately repelled. He'd told me then that he was immune to such things, most likely in a manner similar to Rhoth and some of the outerlanders.

It's a concern I have to raise.

"Hold on," I say, as Zander prepares to step forward. I look directly at my grandfather. "You told me once that mind-manipulation doesn't work on you…"

"And I was absolutely right to tell you that, Brie," he says hurriedly. "It's true. I can repel Mind-Manipulators if I so choose. However, I can quite easily open my mind for exploration too. I am more than happy to do so now. Please, young man, step before me and take a look. Then perhaps you'll all be willing to trust me."

Zander looks to Lady Orlando. My grandmother – *our* grandmother – nods.

My brother moves into position. And the exploration begins.

CHAPTER THREE

It's an entirely unusual sight, watching my brother inspect his grandfather's malevolent mind, neither of them knowing who the other really is.

I can see that that's not entirely lost on Lady Orlando either, the two of us catching eyes on several occasions as the mental excavation takes place. The rest of us merely sit or stand in silence, most likely wondering just what Zander is seeing in the depths of Cromwell's mind.

I can imagine, having been in many Savants' minds now, that it's a sprawling landscape in there, well ordered and vast. I did manage to dip in during my botched assassination attempt, and recall seeing a place of immeasurable intellect. It will, no doubt, take Zander some time to fully collect a decent impression of just what Cromwell's thoughts are on all of this.

Yet, I maintain the suspicion that this is just for show. That he can, if he so desires it, close off certain portions of his mind, conceal them from my brother as he goes searching. Is he merely showing us what we want to see? Or is this really a man who has been forced to go to plan B? A man who has seen his designs for the future dashed, and now will genuinely want to build one alongside us?

Of course, that would never be possible. We will never change our opinions on the world, and I'm fairly sure he'll never change his either. And whatever Zander might find, or whatever he might tell us, I feel fairly certain that he still wishes revenge on us for what we've done. That he will, if and when this force is defeated, look to gain the upper hand once more, and see his remaining Savants prosper in the remains of his new world.

The presence of Agent Romelia Woolf also serves to unnerve me. She sits, watching each us like a hawk, eyes coolly passing from one to the next and working up a picture of how each of us are feeling. And, if ever she manages to catch eyes with one of us, she'll no doubt sneak right in and attempt to read our thoughts too.

In fact, given how she once managed to get Adryan to try to kill me with little more than a glance, I consider it best if we all avoid eye contact with her completely. So I inform the rest to do so, and Adryan and I share a knowing look. And though I don't look into her ice-cold eyes, I do see that smirk of hers rise a little higher.

My brother takes a little over ten minutes before he withdraws from Cromwell's mind, a long enough stretch to make a fairly accurate assessment of his wishes.

As he begins to stir, we all sit up and take notice as he turns to us with a flat expression.

Before he begins, Lady Orlando speaks.

"Artemis, please could you and Agent Woolf leave the room for a few minutes." It's not a request, but an order.

Cromwell nods, stands, and exits the room alongside his sidekick.

Only once he's gone does Zander address us.

"He's telling the truth," he asserts. "Firstly, there *is* an advance force incoming that will be here very soon. They appear to be well ordered and organised and it looks like negotiation might be off the cards…"

"Well of course that's what you'd find in his head," says Beckett. "I don't doubt that the Director believes that, given his stance…"

"It's more than that, Beckett," says Zander. "The Consortium do know a good deal more than us about these people. And yes, they *are* coming to destroy us, not to barter for some sort of peace. We have no choice but to fight back and engage early, as Director Cromwell suggested."

I wonder, as I listen, whether Zander rather likes the idea. In some ways, I wouldn't consider him the most reliable man for the job when determining whether war is necessary or not, given his obsession and need for battle.

Or maybe I'm just being ultra paranoid. It's so difficult to tell these days…

"And his designs for us?" questions Rycard. "I assume you found no hidden plot to destroy us or betray us in this pact?"

Zander shakes his head.

"Nothing like that," he says. "Though, we can't rule it out either. It does appear that his primary function right now is to provide sanctuary for the Savants in the city and protect them. They are his priority, but beyond that, he appears to harbour no real grudge against the City Guards who joined our cause, or the people in general."

"Well, he wouldn't, would he?" says Rycard. "Warped as his thinking is, he's at least consistent in wishing to proliferate the Savants. Seeing as so many have now been killed, he'll need the rest of the people to help rebuild. The landscape is totally different now. And, well, he's a Savant, so only thinks logically. I don't think he'll desire revenge over us or anything like that. What do you think, Lady Orlando? You know him better than all of us put together."

She considers it for a second before speaking.

"I agree with what you just said, Rycard. Artemis wishes to grow the Savant population, and that hasn't changed. And yes, he'll need regular Enhanced and Unenhanced to help do that now, more than ever before. So, yes, defending the city will be his top priority. And given his current stance, creating a peaceful pact between us would appear to be the most logical way forward. Is that what you saw in his mind, Zander?"

My brother nods.

"Pretty much, yeah."

"Well then, the immediate focus for us is clear – we need to think about destabilising this forward unit. Zander, what else did you find out about them?"

"Not much more than what he told us. He certainly has scouts posted towards the edges of the western woods and beyond. The smaller force looks, as he said, to be a couple of hundred strong, and are certainly no negotiation party. They'll likely be here by tonight. We don't have much time to debate this."

"Tonight?" gasps Beckett. "Well that hardly gives us a chance to prepare."

"No, it doesn't," says Lady Orlando. "It would appear that this new war has come to us quicker than expected."

"So what's the plan?" questions Beckett. "You confirm that we're to operate alongside Cromwell's Stalkers?"

Somewhat begrudgingly, my grandmother nods.

"We have no choice." She turns to Freya. "Get him back in."

Freya marches to the door, opens it up, and Cromwell returns along with Woolf. He retakes his seat calmly, seeming fully aware of what's just gone on within the room.

"How many Stalkers do you have, Artemis?" Lady Orlando asks.

He rubs his chin in thought.

"Hmmmm, how many is it, Romelia? A little under two hundred I believe."

"Yes, Director Cromwell," says Woolf. "One hundred and eighty six."

"There you have it, Cornelia."

"And how many are you planning on sending to ambush this advance force?"

"I'd say about fifty of my better ones should do it."

"You don't think you should use more?" she queries.

"Well, you know my Stalkers. Killing machines. I'm assuming, of course, that you'll match that number with your own hybrids?"

Lady Orlando looks to Beckett.

"That would be most of our elites," Beckett says. "It seems rather dangerous risking them all."

"Needs must, Mr Beckett," says Cromwell. "There are hundreds and hundreds of City Guards in the city, and many, many more of your own soldiers. I also have thousands of Con-Cops. We have more than enough to defend the walls, but if we merely allow them to walk through the woods without impediment, the challenge will be greater. My people calculate that defeating this smaller force will vastly weaken their main assault…"

"Then add more of your Stalkers to the cause," says Beckett. "Why supply only fifty when you know there are two hundred or more soldiers incoming, potentially very powerful ones?"

"Because, as I say, my men are perfectly capable of dealing with this threat, as long as you supply the same number. Yes, they will have some powerful men with them, but our combined force of hybrids, on either side, will overwhelm them in these lands. After all, they are lands we know well, and they do not. Now come, Cornelia, let us make this decision and move on. They are coming, and coming fast."

"Fine, fifty of yours and fifty of ours," decides Lady Orlando swiftly. "We'll eliminate them and, if a chance to do so arises, will seek to negotiate with their leaders when they arrive. I will not completely discount the possibility of diplomacy, despite what you say. However, it appears that we'll need to strike first of all."

As Cromwell's teeth appear beneath a half-smile, Lady Orlando turns once more to Beckett.

"Return to Inner Haven immediately and gather your men," she says. You know the western woods well. Use the advantage, Beckett, and only engage if you feel you have the upper hand. Retreat if you need to."

Her eyes swing back to Cromwell.

"Who leads your Stalkers?" she asks.

"Colonel Hatcher," he replies.

"He's still alive then," remarks Lady Orlando. "See that he liaises with Beckett. No funny business now, Artemis. We have no choice but to trust you on this."

He nods respectfully, and I feel the lurching sickness in the depths of my gut begin to rumble. I feel I have to be there too.

"What about me? And Zander?" I ask.

My grandmother might, I suspect, wish to keep us safe from all this. Though, I'm sure she knows that's not possible. Zander, in particular, needs to be at the front and centre of any fight, despite the injury to his shoulder that won't get much time to recover now.

"I require something different of you two," she informs us. "You say, Zander, that Rhoth remains resolute in his position and refuses to leave the woods?"

My brother nods.

"Well then, this presents both problem and opportunity. Let's focus on the latter. Go to Rhoth again, both of you, and seek his aid. If he's to defend his lands, then that's fine. We can use his knowledge of the woods and abilities as a hunter and trapper."

"He was injured during the fight with Bjorn, Lady Orlando," I say. "He might not be in much of a position to fight."

"Then take medicine," she says immediately. "We can ill afford Rhoth falling into enemy hands. He has too much knowledge of us now and could be used against us. Let's make him an asset instead."

I nod, and so does Zander. I didn't think it would happen this fast, but I'm rather happy to be heading out to warn Rhoth and the Fangs of what's coming. They have become quite dear to me.

"Freya and Rycard, you two will continue to arrange the forces at home and bolster the city's defences. And Artemis, make sure you order your loyal City Guards to help."

"Oh, I will Cornelia. Worry not."

"And where will you go?" she queries.

"Well, for now I'll return to the REEF. However, once this force has been dealt with, I'll require sanctuary within the city walls. The REEF is a fortress, but not one capable of withstanding an attack of thousands. My Stalkers will prove their worth. I hope that will satisfy you and show you my loyalty to this mutual cause of ours?"

A shiver runs up my spine at his words. He's slithering back through the door…

"We'll speak once it's done," says Lady Orlando dispassionately. "I can make no other promise than that."

An equally impassive expression marches onto Cromwell's face. And with that, the meeting ends.

CHAPTER FOUR

As Cromwell heads off back out of the gate along with Woolf, the rest of us remain behind for a brief few moments. Once more, our leader reiterates the need for haste to all of us, before sending Adryan, Beckett, Rycard and Freya from the room, all of them ready to be quickly returned to the city to continue their duties.

Alone now with only my grandmother and brother, I wonder if she's about to reveal who she is to him. She sways her eyes over us affectionately, and delays a moment before speaking. When she does, her voice is soft.

"How's the shoulder, Zander?" she asks.

My brother stiffens.

"Fine," he announces stoically.

"I'm not asking too much of you, am I?" she queries, glancing at both of us. "I forget sometimes how young you both are."

Zander seems almost insulted by the insinuation.

"You could ask plenty more, Lady Orlando, and it still wouldn't be enough. I'm happy to serve this cause, and to serve you, whatever the task may be."

She smiles and reaches out, cupping his cheek with her wrinkled palm.

"My dear boy, I don't deserve you. Either of you," she adds, looking to me. "I…"

She trails off and looks away, before recomposing herself.

"You're well rested?" she asks.

We both nod.

"And you have everything you need?"

She scans us, fully armoured and armed with our pulse rifles, sidearms, knives, grenades, and all manner of goodies.

"We are, Lady Orlando," confirms Zander.

She frowns a little at the official title and shakes her head. Once more, I think she might tell Zander the truth. But once more, she refuses the urge.

"You can call me Cornelia if you wish," she says. "My name is no secret now."

"Um…if that's what you want," says Zander, rather rigidly.

She shakes her head.

"Only if *you* want," she says. Then she waves her hand and looks to the door. "It doesn't matter," she mutters. "You should probably get going sooner rather than later. You know where Rhoth's village is?"

"I do."

"Then go to him. At least, even if he chooses not to help, you'll give him some warning. I think Rhoth has earned that, with all he's done to aid us."

"I agree," I say avidly.

"And the others?" asks Zander.

"Beckett will arrange attack and ambush plans for our men, and will work closely with Colonel Hatcher. The Colonel is a staunch military man, and isn't dissimilar to Beckett as it happens. They should be able to work together just fine."

"Right. We'll join then in the fight whether Rhoth is with us or not," says Zander. "I'll contact him on the radio."

Lady Orlando nods silently. Ever since I discovered her true identity, she's seemed, in my eyes at least, to have grown averse to putting either of us in unnecessary danger.

"And this Colonel Hatcher?" I ask. "Is he a Stalker as well?"

Lady Orlando nods.

"In title, I suppose, though he's more than that. He'll make a useful ally for the time being."

"Yeah, he's a ruthless commander," adds Zander. "Let's hope that Beckett puts his animosity aside for the time being."

"He will," confirms Lady Orlando. "Beckett speaks his mind and that's a good thing, but when the time comes and the decision is made, he'll see it done."

"So...this is really happening," I say, looking to the both of them. "We're fighting *with* the Stalkers. With Cromwell. I mean, that's weird for me, and I've only been on the scene for a few months. It must be ultra odd for the both of you..."

"War is odd, Brie," says Lady Orlando, nodding. "Sometimes you need to compromise, even with an enemy, if it serves the greater good. Believe me, I wish there was another way out of this, but so far Artemis has been good on his word. We know full well that our history has been...troubled...but personal issues need to be swept to one side at times like this."

She turns her focus specifically on me as she speaks, as if offering warning to continue to keep her secrets. Zander peers with some interest, though I know full well that he won't be reading her thoughts. Unlike me, he refuses to do so on friends and....family.

"I guess," I concede, hating that fact. "I still don't trust him, though."

"And nor should you. You may deal with the devil, but you don't have to trust him. All of us must continue to be vigilant at times like this. But alas, time is becoming a problem. So you must go. Good luck, you wonderful pair. I'll see you back in the city soon."

We leave the small barracks to the side of the gate, and Lady Orlando heads for her escort to be returned to Inner Haven. The garrison of soldiers at the western gate remains large, and work continues

39

to be done to strengthen the city's defences. I look upon it all and consider that no army would attempt to breach the gates, so well defended as they are, not when so many sections of the wall remain far more exposed.

"When this army gets here, they're not gonna come this way," I say, looking out upon the gate.

"*If*," corrects Zander. "If we can stop them at source, we will."

"Sure. But let's say they reach the walls. The city's huge. There's no chance we can protect the entire perimeter."

My brother shakes his head.

"No, there isn't. But we have mobile units capable of moving into position very quickly. And should Outer Haven be breached, we have Inner Haven to fall back to, and that's much easier to defend."

Seeing the worry on my face, he adds, "It won't come to that, Brie. I know we've seen some strange people with strange powers recently, but I can't imagine that this entire army is filled with them. Hybrids are rare, and they won't have the weaponry we do. And you know what, I've fought the Stalkers for years…I know just how much of an asset they'll be. I'm sure this army is made up of regular soldiers, maybe even mostly Unenhanced. I reckon they have no idea what they're getting themselves into."

He smiles weakly and lays an arm over my shoulder, pulling me into an abbreviated, brotherly hug.

"I'll always be there to protect you," he says, kissing my forehead. "Now come on, let's go see the big man…again!"

As we move off through the gate, and the wilds present themselves before me once more, I review his words and know that they're designed to sooth my concerns. Because really, my brother isn't so naïve as to believe what he's just said. If this army are coming, then they're coming for a reason and know just what they're up against.

Call me paranoid, but I'm not quite so optimistic.

CHAPTER FIVE

According to my brother, the main village of the Fangs is deep in the western woods and quite difficult to find. Though the Fangs tend to move around occasionally, using hunting lodges whilst tracking prey and gathering food for winter and times of hardship, they maintain a permanent station in a secret grove, well concealed among the rocks at the heart of the forest.

I put it to Zander that Rhoth is surely safe if the village is so well hidden. His retort is that, with an army of upwards of ten thousand passing straight through, he might well be stumbled upon.

Moreover, Rhoth isn't the type to cower and hide with the women and children. In fact, from what I've heard, the women and children of the Fangs are fine warriors themselves. Growing up under perpetual threat from the beasts, Shadows, rival tribes, and natural forces of the wilds would certainly serve to make the people hardy, regardless of gender and age.

Rhoth did tell us, belligerent as he is, that he'd defend his lands if he needed to. Zander was pretty adamant that he'd be overrun, and while Rhoth is clearly a fine leader and commander, he might be slightly ignorant of just what we're facing. He might be able to defend his lands against an onslaught from the Bear-Skins or Skullers, but an army of thousands would quickly destroy him and his entire tribe should they have the mind to do so.

And, while the village is well hidden, it's quite possible that it's also well known. After all, if this army from the west have been sending in scouts to watch over Haven, they're sure to have learned all about the surrounding tribes as well. If they know where the Fangs live, then they'll either choose to parlay with them and bring them into the fold, ignore them, or destroy them on their path to Haven. Only one of those options sounds good to me.

With the morning taken by our discussions with Cromwell, the afternoon quickly gets underway as we trek through the wilds. We travel at as speedy a pace as we can through the thickening thickets, clogged up with tangled trees and only occasionally breaking into little clearings and more sparsely populated groves.

It's a good time of day for it. With the sun bright and casting its light through the foliage, the lurking beasts of the wild are mostly kept at bay. It's a nocturnal place, where the creeping creatures seek darkness and gloom to strike. Dusk is when they begin to stir, though storms that blot out the light also tend to bring them out of their slumber.

Now, though, Zander tells me we're quite able to operate without too much fear of an attack. That's especially the case as we work fairly close to the REEF, where the Stalkers are likely to be scouting and thus scaring away the local fauna.

Oddly, knowing that there might well be little patrols of Stalkers nearby puts me on edge more than anything the wilderness might throw up. Ever since being brought into the fold, it's the black-clad hybrids who cause the most concern in me. It's a habit that's grown and is having trouble being broken, worrying that one of them might leap from the trees and attempt to strike us down.

That concern hasn't been completely assuaged by this temporary pact. I still can't shake the idea that Cromwell's up to something.

"So what was it like in his head," I ask my brother as we work our way west. "Cromwell, I mean."

"Same as most Savants really," says Zander. "You know what it's like."

"Yeah. So what, no demons and monsters lurking in there. That's kinda what I imagine the inside of his mind to be like. Lakes of molten lava and pits of pain and torture. You know, hell…"

"A nightmare, basically?"

"Exactly," I say.

He laughs.

"Well, nothing like that. His desire to serve and save the Savants is clear and profound. It's what drives him more than anything."

"Really? I would have thought his ego would be doing that."

"Savants don't really have egos, though, do they?

They serve a function and perform a duty. It just so happens that Director Cromwell's is to build the profile of his people, same as us. His methods are, well, questionable. But then, Savants hardly care for that."

"They sure don't. Not all of them anyway. Lady Orlando or Adryan would never do what Cromwell's done. Nor would Burns, or loads of others I assume."

"Well, yeah there's a spectrum of empathy, obviously. Then again, we're not so different. Lady Orlando did order the High Tower to be destroyed, and most of us were perfectly happy to see it fall. He kills us…we kill them. No one's really innocent."

"I guess not. But let's not compare crimes. I mean, whatever way you look at it, he's been the one who's destroyed so many lives. We're just reacting to that."

"That's true. In a way, we're two very different species now, fighting for dominance when, maybe…we should be working together. Who knows, perhaps Cromwell's seen the light now and seen what we're capable of. Maybe he really does want to work together from now on."

"Pfft, unlikely," I huff. "Surely the idea of that sounds repellent to you? You've worked for years to topple his regime and free the city…"

"And now we have, partly at least. The city's under our control. We have found some common ground. At the end of the day, Brie, my priority has been in making sure the regular people of the city live free. That's the number one goal ahead of actually killing Cromwell. We've taken out most of the Savants, most of his top leaders. There's no coming back for him now. The question is whether we show mercy and choose to cooperate, or reignite our war once we've dealt with this new threat. Truth be told, we've done more than I ever expected. Nothing is really going according to our original plans, and we all just have to wing it from here on out."

"Well, call me crazy, but I still want that man six feet under…" I grumble.

My brother turns on me, eyes narrow.

"Dismiss that thought, Brie," he warns. "I know what you're like, and can't have you doing something stupid. Remember, the Director is untouchable. If he dies, we'll have everyone converging on us."

I counter with an equally deep frown.

"Zander, what do you take me for? You think I'd what, kill Cromwell or something? Don't be stupid. I know he's untouchable. I'm just saying, if we get out of this alive, then hopefully events transpire that lead to his death....that's all I'm saying."

His glare continues for a moment, and for a second I feel him ready to dart into my thoughts and see them for himself. He refuses the urge, and fills his lungs.

"You really hate him, don't you? More than me.

More than anyone. I wonder why that is…"

"Erm, it's pretty obviously," rushes my voice. "He kept me in the damn High Tower, locked to a chair for days! He was going to recondition me and use me, turn me into a Stalker or something. He's killed and ruined the lives of thousands, tens of thousands of people. And all the people we've lost, you and me and everyone…we've lost them because of him. Yeah, I *hate* him, Zander. I wonder why you don't seem to."

He watches my rant calmly, and I turn my eyes to the mist covered ground.

"I do hate him," he says coolly. "But I don't get overly emotional about it, Brie. You'll learn eventually to suppress such impulses. Here, let me get in your head and calm you down. I'll straighten you out…"

"NO!" I say loudly, stepping back. "I don't want you or anyone in my head again!"

He lifts his hands to calm me.

"All right, just a suggestion. Brie, you need to relax, OK. This isn't the place for such behaviour."

I feel like arguing back, but instead suck in a long breath of filtered air and shut my eyes to ease the growing mania in my mind. When I open them up again, several long moments later, I feel a whole lot better.

"You're right," I admit. "Sorry. This whole topic just boils my blood. You don't…get it, Zander."

"*I* don't get it?" he says, the edges of his voice

suggesting anger. "Look, this is the last thing I'm going to say on the matter, so listen and listen good. I have been fighting this war for years and years. It has consumed me completely, and trust me when I tell you, I've seen and done some terrible things that even you'll never know about. I do worry, sometimes, that I'll never have a normal life when this is all over. But I don't care about that, because I'm a soldier, and this *is* my life. So don't tell me I don't get it, Brie. Don't say that to me again."

His words bristle with resentment as they come. And as they come, I understand just why. I stay silent for a moment once he's finished, slightly cowed by the force of his reaction, before nodding gently and whispering softly.

"I didn't mean…" I start.

He cuts me off, his voice drawing back.

"It's OK. Let's move on and forget it. I understand this is hard for you. I forget how new it all is to you, and I really do get it. But let's just bury this conversation for now. We've got a way to go yet, and can't be distracted out here in the wild. Agreed?"

I nod and lift a mild, slightly uneasy smile.

"Agreed."

We press on into the afternoon, hiking and navigating through these parts a constant challenge. As with our very recent trip up the mountains just north of here, I suspect that Kira was a useful ally in traversing these woods, and Zander needs to stop fairly regularly to assess just where we are and make sure we're headed in the right direction.

For a time, we don't speak, letting the little discussion dissipate in our minds and any heated feelings cool. It takes some time before we share words again, stopping near a stream to catch our bearings and take a short rest.

"How far?" I ask tentatively.

"Shouldn't be too long now," is my brother's non-committal reply. "You feeling OK?"

"Yeah, fine," I say. "How about you? The shoulder giving you any discomfort."

He shakes his head.

"Nah, nothing major. Little bit of trouble with mobility, but that's all. Should loosen up over the course of the next day or two."

We continue with a smattering of slightly strained small-talk, listening to the birds chirping and the stream trickling as it meanders through the forest. Mercifully, our conversation is broken by the sound of static.

Zander reaches immediately for his belt and detaches the mobile radio he has with him. He clicks a button, and speaks.

"This is Zander."

"What's your progress?" comes the hoarse voice of Beckett on the other line.

"Still working towards Rhoth's village. No confirmation yet that he's there. You?"

"Hybrids are gathered," Beckett says. "We're about to move beyond the western gate and meet with Colonel Hatcher and the Stalkers. Plan is to head straight for the western border of the forest and set up traps and watch positions. I'll inform you when I have more information."

"All right, keep me informed. We'll hurry on and see if Rhoth wants to join the fun. Out."

He clicks the radio off and reattaches it to his belt.

"And how far is the village from the border?" I ask. "It's near the middle, right?"

"Closer towards the west, actually. It'll be quicker going on that side. The woods are generally thinner towards the western edge."

"Right, and I guess we can use our Dasher powers if we have to?"

"I'd prefer not to waste energy if we can avoid it. Beckett will travel by wheel for as far as he can go – that'll be towards the REEF – but will have to go the rest of the way on foot. They should have plenty of time to set their positions and form ambushes."

"And presumably there are Stalker scouts off watching this incoming force. You know, seeing what they're armed with et cetera?"

Zander nods.

"We should be well informed of their capabilities. Hopefully they won't expect us to greet them so far from the city."

"Catch them off guard..."

"Precisely."

We jump to our feet and press on, Beckett's update now fuelling us with a little more spring to our step. The inclusion of another voice out here in the wilderness has also served to dismiss any lingering awkwardness due to our previous discussion. It was much needed.

With the shape of the earth undulating, with little rises and falls, small hills and mounds peppering the earth, we eventually arrive at a cluster of rocks, set within a small recess in the earth. Through a passage between tightly packed thickets, Zander leads me on, passing tree and stone and eventually working our way towards a hidden clearing.

My brother stops before we venture on, and turns to me.

"The village is just up ahead," he tells me. "It's not walled off like with the Roosters – the natural features do that job for them – but they will have guards set watching the entrance. Let me do the talking, OK."

"Sure. But won't they recognise us?"

"It depends who's on the door. We've make progress with the Fangs in recent weeks, but a lot of them hold no love for me."

"Well, then I think it's my duty to suggest that *I* do the talking," I joke, smirking.

Zander raises a smile.

"Follow me."

CHAPTER SIX

The well-concealed track towards the clearing the Fangs call home ends with a passage between two boulders. On first view, there appears to be nothing unusual about it, and certainly no guard in place. Then, as we creep forward with our pulse rifles on our backs and masks removed from our faces, a voice crackles from the foliage.

"Stop right there. We have half a dozen guns on you right now."

We stop, and I look for the source of the voice. It came from the right, just behind the large boulder by the looks of things. I don't recognise it, though. I've spoken to a fair few of the Fangs by now, but this one seems new to me. Then again, most of Rhoth's hunting party up in the mountains did die in the battle with the Bear-Skins, so there's no surprise in that.

"By your garb you come from the big city with all the lights. State your name and business."

Zander steps a little ahead of me.

"It is Zander of the Nameless and his twin sister, Brie of the same. We come to speak with Rhoth and bring warning."

"Zander…" says the voice quietly. "Our tribe has lost many men in recent days on account of you. I have lost friends…on account of you."

The man steps from behind the boulder, sharp eyes staring. He's well built, quite young, and intense in his countenance.

"It is true, the Fangs have become embroiled with the Nameless recently. We never intended to fight the Bear-Skins, however. That was not on my account."

"Our people only reignited the war with the Bear-Skins on *your* account," counters the tribesman. "In fact, perhaps it is this girl, Brie, who is more to blame. It was she who inspired Bjorn's ire over in his territory as I hear it. What say you, girl?"

I look to Zander for confirmation to speak. He nods.

"I say that I'm sorry for your losses. But I also say that I count Rhoth and the Fangs as friends and allies, and that he would wish for us to pass. We have urgent news that you need to hear, and that you should already be aware of."

"Urgent news? You speak of this barbarian army approaching," says the young man. "We know of this already. You are not the first outsiders to pass this way today. Not even in the last hour…"

"What? What do you mean?" questions Zander fiercely. "Has someone come? Someone from the incoming army?"

The man stares at Zander for a moment but

doesn't speak. Then, from the side, another Fang hurries into view, necklace more readily adorned with an assortment of teeth and claws, face bearded and tanned. He also has a fresh wound down the side of his arm, and I know just why. He was with us only days ago in the mountains. This is a Fang I do know, though his name escapes me.

He steps forward, lifting his hand to wave us on.

"Come, Zander and Brie. You must come now."

"But I am master of the gate today," growls the first, younger man.

The older man stares him down.

"Then stay at the gate, Henrik. These twins are our friends, and they are permitted entry. Come," he says, turning his eyes on us once more.

We don't need a third invite. Stepping forward, we march on down the track as the younger man called Henrik sets about reiterating his authority once more. He's shot down again, the older man clearly ranking above him in the village – his necklace makes that apparent if nothing else - and eventually concedes as we press on past him and set our eyes on the settlement ahead.

It's very unlike the one occupied by the Roosters. Here, all huts and shacks are built more traditionally on the ground, the entire clearing surrounded by natural formations of rocks and thick woods, with the canopy above cleared and presenting the sun an opportunity to bathe the village in its natural yellow light.

It's larger than I thought it would be as well, stretching away quite far and clearly calling home to several hundred tribespeople at least. While Rhoth lost a few dozen men only days ago, his stocks are still fairly well supplied.

As we move into the village, Zander speaks.

"What's happening, Larsson?" he questions. "This other guest...who is it?"

The Fang named Larsson stops in his tracks and lowers his voice.

"You were right at the gate," he says. "It's a man from the barbarian horde, an envoy. He's come to treat with Rhoth."

"What do you mean?" I ask hurriedly. "To what, strike a deal or something?"

Larsson shakes his head.

"I know not," he says. "Rhoth is speaking with him alone. No one else is permitted entry. I didn't like the look of the man when he entered. I fear he might be trying to influence Rhoth. It's good you've come, Zander. You can stop this madness. We shouldn't sell our souls to this devil horde..."

"OK," says Zander, "lead on Larsson. Take us to them immediately."

We press on, passing a number of different sized huts, all scantily built from strips of wood, branches, leaves and other natural materials. I see hunters lingering about, much like those I've met before. And the women as well, lacking the jewellery that adorns the men's necks. Instead, they have fang earrings and bracelets, and the children too appear wild and draped in their little furs and pelts.

They all stare as we pass through, whispering to each other. It must be a strange day indeed to have so many guests appear here within their hidden village, Zander and me particularly interesting for how we're dressed and the glowing pulse rifles that sit fixed to our backs.

In the centre of the village, the largest shack of all is situated. Octagonal in shape and a little more grand than the others, it appears to be some sort of meeting point, a village hall of sorts. Outside, I see additional guards with their old, rusted rifles and spears, a strange amalgamation of the ancient and modern - relatively speaking at least, seeing as their guns are old enough to be considered antiques.

I don't recognise either of them as they set their eyes on us.

"I need to speak with Rhoth immediately," says Larsson.

The men look at him and then us. One of them answers.

"Rhoth doesn't wish to be disturbed. He is in talks with…"

"Yes, I know, that's just why I'm here. Zander of the Nameless brings news. Now step aside, and let us pass."

The men look to each other and then at my brother. It seems he continues to be a rather divisive figure around these parts, which isn't surprising given the history between the Fangs and the Nameless. We may have somewhat endeared ourselves to Rhoth and his hunting party recently, but the remainder of the tribe appears less convinced.

Unfortunately, my part in all of this has spread as well, and I'm right there in the same boat alongside him. The presence of Larsson, however, is a blessing. As one of the few Fangs to have been present with us during recent excursions, he's an ally here in what appears to be quite an inhospitable place.

"I will…take this news to Rhoth," says one of the guards. "Wait here a moment."

He steps inside the hut, moving through a doorway made from hanging vines and jingling fangs. My eyes once more peruse the village and watching faces as he goes.

"Is West around?" I ask Larsson, searching for my new friend.

"He's been down at the river hunting fish," I'm told. "He should return shortly."

Within the hut, I hear a familiar growl that I know to be Rhoth's voice. All goes silent as we listen. A few moments later, the guard returns looking a little sheepish.

"He doesn't wish to see you," announces the guard. "He's in a…foul mood."

I watch Zander's lips curl down and his eyes narrow. He locks his gaze on the guard who seems to fall into a sudden reverie, before blinking a few times as a frown descends over his eyes. He shakes his head.

"I…I apologise," he mutters, drawing a confused gaze from his fellow guard. "I meant to say, Rhoth will be happy to see you. Please, go ahead."

The other guard seems to grow increasingly perplexed with every word. Meanwhile, Zander merely glances at me and drops a wink. I smile back, considering it lucky he picked out a guard who's susceptible to his mental manipulations. Around here, I know that's quite hit and miss.

"Thank you very much," says Zander magnanimously, stepping towards the door of hanging vines as Larsson and I follow quickly behind him.

We enter into a dark and quite humid place, carpeted with all sorts of furs and pelts and with a fire in the centre that spills smoke up through a gap in the roof. The flickering light gives form to the large shape of Rhoth, sitting on a chair fashioned from the trunk of a tree, a number of gashes painting his skin from recent battles.

Across from him, a man of much smaller proportions sits in a similar chair. He has short brown hair, a smattering of uneven stubble, and a set of armour that looks strangely familiar. My eyes slant at the sight of him, and a snarl works itself onto my face. Our counterpart's expression takes on a similar form as he turns his eyes on my brother and me.

"What…why are you here?" he says suddenly, as if he's in command.

Looking at Rhoth, I consider that he might well be. The leader of the Fangs, I know, isn't prone to falling under the spells of Mind-Manipulators. Yet today it appears that something has gone awry on that front. Larsson may well have been right.

The old Fang looks to his head tribesman now, and steps forward.

"Rhoth, are you OK? You appear…not yourself."

Rhoth's eyes look glassy, tired. He lifts his head and nods.

"I'm fine…just fine, Larsson. You shouldn't be here. I told the guard not to admit you." His eyes find Zander and me. "And what are you doing here?" he sighs exasperatedly. "Why can't I be rid of you…"

"Who are these people, Rhoth?" questions the envoy, his voice deep and rhythmic, as if enough to put you under a spell all on its own. He looks upon us closely. "Ah, you're from the big city with all the lights I see. Your armour, your weapons. Yes, it is true. Part of the Nameless to take control of the city, no doubt. Don't look so surprised. We know more about you than you think."

"And *we* is?" growls Zander.

The man smiles but doesn't answer. He looks back to Rhoth.

"Are we to continue our negotiation, Rhoth?" he asks. "These people shouldn't be here."

"And why's that?" I say loudly. "So you can work your mental magic. Yeah, I can see what you're doing. Rhoth, you're not yourself. This man is trying to trick you."

"Trick me?" says Rhoth angrily, standing to his feet. "No one tricks me, girl. You…you know this!"

"Larsson is right," I go on. "You're not yourself."

"I am myself!" he growls. "Now get out of here. Guards!"

The guards hustle quickly through the doorway, guns primed. I hold up one hand to calm them.

"It's OK…it's all good," I say. "Things are fine, don't do anything stupid now."

"Stupid was you coming here!" says Rhoth. "This is the village of the Fangs. It isn't a place for people from the big city. Now go. Get out of here!"

He seems far more manic than usual, his limbs twitching, nostrils flaring. In the other chair, the envoy just sits calmly, a little smile on his face. I know he's to blame. And so does my brother.

He looks at the man now, and I can see him preparing to strike if he has to. This man has clearly come here for a single purpose – to enlist the support of the Fangs, to use his tricks to get them to either fight or reveal what they know about us.

His presence here says a lot. It tells us that this is no rabble approaching. It confirms that they know far more than we might have thought. They are clearly aware of Rhoth and the Fangs, and even have knowledge of where this village is. Who knows, perhaps one of the Fangs has been a spy all alone, feeding information to the west. Whatever the case, we cannot leave this place with this man still here.

And my brother knows it.

As he prepares to make his move, however, I hear more commotion outside. Suddenly, through the door another figure comes, and I look upon the youthful form of West, striding in with a narrow gaze that immediately falls upon the stranger to these parts, sitting casually in his tree trunk chair.

The expression that slowly builds on his face is one I've never seen. There's a depth to it, a pool of hurtful memory that seems to bubble up through every pore. His eyes peruse the man and go stark, and suddenly I know just why his garb looks so familiar.

It is the same sort of armour, old and weather-worn, that adorned the bodies of the men who destroyed West's village all those years ago. The memory I saw in his mind of his people being massacred, his parents killed, now strikes again. And before I know it, or can do anything to stop it, West surges straight for the man with a roar of fury, drawing a knife from his belt as he goes.

I have no time to react, and nor does anyone else except Rhoth, standing right there beside the messenger, who looks suddenly frightened as the young Fang pours forward with murder in his eyes.

Rhoth hurls himself across just in time, grappling with West and taking hold of his wrist before the knife can plunge deep into the envoy's flesh. The man stands and staggers backwards, and West wriggles like a fish in Rhoth's mighty grasp.

And though he's spent his life here a mute, only speaking on such rare occasions, now he suddenly finds his voice, roaring loud.

"It was him! His people! They killed my family! They destroyed my village! It was him!"

His voice fills the air, cracking through overuse when it's so rarely deployed. It's so loud that, beyond the hut, the villagers must hear, bodies drawing closer to the central shack to see what all the fuss is about.

He calls again and again, his voice slowly growing weaker and his struggling limbs ceasing to try to wrest themselves from Rhoth's powerful grip. Yet the great Fang himself now appears to be waking, young West's words breaking him from the spell. His eyes flicker, and his mind fills with the distress of the young man who he took as his son, who he found as a boy, frightened and alone in the wilderness.

I watch, breathless, as the true Rhoth comes back to the fore. He stands tall again, and the crazed look in his eyes is dismissed. He turns to the envoy, cowering against the wall, and his façade curls, framed in fury.

"It was his people?" he asks quietly.

West, panting hard, nods.

"Him…it was him…I know it…."

Rhoth lets West go, and the shack goes still and silent. Then, in a sudden burst, he thrusts himself forward, grabs hold of the messenger, and drags him in front of West.

"Kill him," he growls.

West doesn't need to hear any more.

My brother calls out, "No!" for a reason I don't immediately understand, and the cowardly envoy squeaks in fear and attempts to escape. It's no use. Rhoth is too strong, and West is too quick. His knife comes slashing, right across the man's throat, opening it up wide.

And the shack gets a new coating of dark red blood.

CHAPTER SEVEN

The sight of the envoy dropping to his knees, fingers manically clutching at his neck as it spurts blood, would have made me rather queasy not so long ago.

The fact that I look at it without batting an eyelid says a hell of a lot about my transition from regular, cleaner girl in the western quarter of Outer Haven, to rebel, soldier, and gifted killer. I watch without much feeling at all as he sinks to his knees and splutters and spits, his final moments of life upon him.

In fact, if there is a feeling within me, it's one of both hate and justice. If West is right, then this man is part of the barbarian horde that ransacked his lands. And envoy or not, he deserves everything he's got.

My brother, however, reacts differently.

As the rest of us stand motionless, he immediately darts forward, dropping straight to his knees before the dying man.

"Let him suffer," growls Rhoth, perhaps thinking Zander is trying to help.

It takes a moment to realise that he isn't. He's

merely looking for information.

He does so by quickly grabbing at the man's frantic eyes and wrestling their lids open. It's clearly not easy. With the blood still spilling, the envoy quickly sinks to the floor, gurgling his last as his eyes go dead. Soon enough, he's completely motionless, lifeless. I consider that Zander's missed his shot.

I seem to be wrong on that account. He continues to work, holding the now-dead man's eyes open as they stare up and go glassy. We all watch as he slips into the messenger's head for what must be about twenty or so seconds, before grimacing and withdrawing and shouting, "Damn!"

He stands to his feet, shaking his head.

"He was dead," I say. "How could you…"

"There's always brain activity for a short while after death," he grunts. "I had a bit of time."

"And…what did you see?"

He turns to me, eyes haunted.

"Nothing good. Snippets, bare details. But enough…"

"Enough for what?" I ask, breathless.

"To tell us Cromwell was right," he says. "The army is ten thousand strong at least. They're here to destroy us and nothing more. It's what they do – they spread from place to place, destroying villages and settlements, gathering enhanced and hybrids to their cause, stealing and looting rations and whatever resources they need to keep on going."

He turns to West, whose own eyes are still little more than slits, the memory of his past still playing before them.

"Your village…it *was* them," he confirms. "They've been doing this for years, building their strength. Only now are they powerful enough to strike at their main target."

"Haven," I whisper.

My brother nods.

"They call themselves the *Cure*," he growls. "A cure for what they see as weakness in this world. But really they're a plague, ravaging lands and taking what they want. I fear they're far more powerful than we thought…"

"What do you mean? More Enhanced and hybrids?" I query.

Zander nods.

"I think that even Director Cromwell might be underestimating them. This incoming force of two hundred…they're some of their finest warriors. And the rest aren't mere Unenhanced. Their ranks are filled with killers."

"You got all this from his mind?" questions Rhoth, still escaping the spell the envoy had over him.

Zander turns to him.

"That, and more, Rhoth," he says. "The man had a telepathic link to someone in the main army. I heard him speak to him with his final thoughts."

"And what did he say?" growls Rhoth.

"He said he'd failed. That you and the Fangs were not with them. I'm sorry, Rhoth. He said…you needed to be destroyed."

The big man stiffens and grunts.

"Destroy us?! Nothing of the sort will happen. Not here in *my* woods. I will defend them till I die."

"And those that can't fight?" asks Zander. "They know where the village is. They'll ransack it just as they have so many others. All your people will be killed. Please, Rhoth, clear out from here. You cannot stay."

The great Fang looks to West, then to Larsson, and the guards lingering by the door.

"Zander is right," says Larsson. "Those who can fight, should do so. But the rest need to be safe, Rhoth."

"Haven," I say. "We will protect them in Haven. There's nowhere else…"

"There are plenty of other places, girl," growls Rhoth. "Maybe Kervan and the Roosters will give them sanctuary."

"And you think these people…the Cure…you think they won't know about the Roosters? They know about us all, Rhoth. The Nameless, the Consortium, Haven, and the tribes. Perhaps they'll be safe in the mountains, but perhaps not. Are you willing to take that risk? There's nowhere safer than

Haven. If you really care about the safety of your people, you'll send them to the city immediately."

Zander's words leave behind a short silence, the challenge to Rhoth laid down. He doesn't seem to enjoy being spoken to in such a manner, least of all here in his village. But as a good leader, he needs to see reason. And I'm relieved when his fierce eyes begin to soften, and his great, bearded chin dips into a nod.

"Maybe you're right, boy," he says.

It's enough of a concession for my brother to let out a breath.

He turns his eyes back to Larsson.

"Spread the word, Lars," he says. "The people are to make for the big city with all the lights. All hunters and fighters must assemble. We will not present this barbarian horde free passage through our lands."

As Larsson nods and moves towards the exit, Zander asks, "Is that sensible, Rhoth? You've done enough fighting already. You should go with your people and protect them."

A gurgle of laughter creeps up Rhoth's throat.

"Boy, I appreciate your words. But you will never understand how we operate here. We will war with these people, as you are. They come to destroy us all, as you say. We are all allies in this fight."

Zander smiles.

"I do understand, Rhoth. You want to protect your

lands and your home. I understand that full well."

"Then question me not," crackles the tribesman's voice. "But do you part instead – call your friends in Haven, tell them my people are coming and need tending. Put those you trust to the task, Zander. Do that for me."

"Of course. I will, Rhoth. They'll be well seen to."

"Good." He turns to West and lays a hand on his shoulder. "Revenge, West. We will finally have it."

I see the two men smile at each other, but can only think that they'll both die this night. I may well be in that boat too, and Zander. All of us, in fact, might see our ends when the light fades and the moon rises. But once again, such a thing fails to faze me. The threat of death is something I'm quickly learning to live with.

And so far, I've met the challenge.

For the next half hour, the camp heaves and rushes. Stepping outside the main hut, I see some dissent and questioning among the people, the likes of Henrik, abandoning his post at the gate, chief among the doubters. Yet with Rhoth, West, Larsson, and the guards who witnessed what happened singing from the same song sheet, all concerns are swiftly put to bed.

They may have a great deal of distrust for Zander, the Nameless, and the city of Haven, but they have no choice but to trust in their leader. We are, it seems, the lesser of two evils, and the city of Haven that they have long feared now looks set to become their sanctuary, to live up to its very name.

As the old, young, and those unable to fight gather their belongings and ready themselves for the trek, I get a good idea of the true numbers here. There are many more than I thought there would be, hundreds now readying themselves for the long march through the woods towards the one place they never thought they'd tread.

Those capable of fighting gather their weapons too, not only men but a good number of women amongst them. A few will go with the rest to offer protection through the woods, but most appear ready and willing to defend the woods with their lives.

Zander, meanwhile, gets on the radio and calls it in, making sure that the soldiers at the gate are prepared to escort them into the city. I ask him just who he'll trust to help them settle in, and he mentions Sophie as an option given her experience of the Fangs when travelling to the mines.

"Good idea," I say to him. "Though, she'll need a good deal of help in arranging them all."

"She'll get it," says Zander. "They'll put the Fangs up somewhere in Outer Haven for now, close to the walls of Inner Haven. If needs be, they can be transported right to the centre."

"You mean, if they city comes under siege, and the walls are breached."

Zander nods.

The rush continues, and soon enough the afternoon is bustling along at a fierce enough pace to suggest that the sun will set before too long and the moon will take its place. I watch my brother pace and grow frustrated, and find that he's having trouble getting through to Beckett.

"There's some sort of interference," he tells me when I ask him what the trouble is.

"Distance?" I ask. "Are we too far from him?"

"I wouldn't have thought so. We're further from Haven and I'm having no trouble speaking with them. Could be that he's got his radio off or it's damaged or…"

"Or what?"

"I don't know. Maybe the Cure have some sort of disruptor technology with them to prevent radio signals from getting through. If so, they're probably getting close. We can't delay much longer, sis. Beckett needs to know what we're facing."

"You're worried," I assert, looking into his eyes. "You think Beckett and Colonel Hatcher are outmatched?"

"I can't be sure. I only got snippets from the envoy's head, but this forward unit is more powerful than we thought. And they have numbers, Brie. We can't afford to lose fifty of our best hybrids, and fifty Stalkers right now. We think we're ambushing them…but maybe it's the other way around."

"Well then, we go? We have our Dasher powers. Rhoth can catch up if he's so keen on fighting. They'll only slow us down, Zander."

He considers it, and looks at the sky.

"I'll speak with Rhoth. See where he's at…"

He rushes off, the village now beginning to clear of those heading for Haven, leaving behind a smaller force of a hundred or so hunters of varying capabilities. I imagine that a lot of Rhoth's finer warriors were part of the hunting group I've spent plenty of time with, many of them losing their lives several days ago in the mountains.

The remainder might just be out of their depth, though it doesn't show in their eyes. Here, in these woods – *their* woods – with this toxic mist that seems to mute the abilities of so many Enhanced and hybrids, the playing field is more level. They are, I know, a great boon to our cause.

As I stand and await my brother's orders, West meanders over to me.

"Revenge, Brie," he says, his voice running free. "I will finally have revenge."

I smile at him, but don't offer any words to douse his flames. No words of worry that he won't get revenge, that he might well fall instead. No words to make him doubt himself, or those he has fought with for years. Instead, I merely nod, and add my flames to his.

"Yes, you will," I say assertively. "For your village, for your people."

He holds my gaze longer than he usually would. So shy at his core, he's been set loose by the promise of blood, buoyed by the life of the envoy he's just taken. And even now, I see the spray of crimson across his clothes from the messenger's neck, war paint for the battle to come.

"And you?" he says. "When will your revenge come? For your father, Maxwell, and your mother, Elisa…"

His words cause a sharp jump in my heart-rate, recalling my parents' names. And as he utters them, I notice Zander nearby, standing with Rhoth, listening as the big man speaks.

I turn back to West, who stares at me, awaiting a response.

"One day," I say. "But this is your night, West. Mine will come…"

"It will," he says confidently. "We will all have our moment."

He heaves in a breath, seeming older and larger than ever before, and from the corner of my eyes I see Zander marching back over.

"Rhoth needs you, West," he says to the young Fang.

West drops a final smile for me before slipping away, leaving me alone with Zander. He looks at me curiously for a moment, before opening his mouth.

"Rhoth is about ready to go. We will go with him at first. He knows the way better than I do, and it's better to go a little slower and save our energy, than waste it and get lost along the path."

"Makes sense," I say.

"I'll keep trying Beckett as we go. By now they're

sure to be in position." He looks to the sky. "It's getting on. No time to waste."

Before he can move off, I draw him back with a query that's been bubbling up in my mind.

"You said the envoy has a telepathic link with someone in the main army," I say. "How did you tap into that? I didn't know that was possible…"

His face takes on an expression of marginal guilt. The realisation doesn't take long to dawn in my mind.

"You…lied?" I whisper, frowning. "There was no link?"

He peers about.

"I said what I needed to say, Brie," he tells me. "We can't risk Rhoth staying here. It's too dangerous for the Fangs, and you know how belligerent he is. They'd either be destroyed, or assimilated into the Cure's army. I did what I had to do to stop that from happening."

"I see…"

"You don't agree?" he questions.

"I, um…no, I do agree, actually. I think you're right. You had to do it."

He smiles, seeming surprised.

"Good. Then you really are learning. And you really are changing. Not long ago, you'd have reprimanded me for such a thing."

I shrug.

"Yep. That girl's dead, though. You did the right thing, brother. You've probably just saved the entire village, and got the hunters to fight alongside us rather than against us. Just…probably best to keep that one from Rhoth, right?"

We glance at the big man, delivering a rousing speech to his assembled warriors.

"Yeah, I'd say that's probably a good idea," he chuckles.

And moving towards the group, we prepare to set off towards the west.

CHAPTER EIGHT

The light in the woods is beginning to fade.

Under the canopy above, the onset of darkness always comes early, the foliage drowning the forest floor below in a deepening gloom. My eyes can penetrate it easily enough, but though the Fangs have no such ocular augmentations, they're capable of operating here within the low light with a surprising ease and skill.

As forest dwellers, the varying states of darkness are common to them, and their eyes have adjusted accordingly. I've seen it all before, and know that, though they are technically Unenhanced, life here in the woods has given them somewhat superhuman senses. They are, in some respects, all hybrids here, with the ability to see, hear, and smell far better than most.

They are fleet of foot too, scurrying quickly through the brush and with a silence that is highly impressive. As we go, I'm almost forced to dial up my Dasher powers, such is the speed with which they travel.

All senses remain alert. With the light fading, and dusk quickly approaching, the beasts of the wild will begin to stake their claim. Eyes search and ears listen, and nostrils continue to pick out the scents given off by their woodland enemies. But with such a force, few beasts will be likely to attack, and the Shadows that lurk in the trees and areas of swamp will no doubt choose to stay away.

But while Rhoth and his hunters are adept at searching for danger, they are also quite skilled at luring it in. As I jog alongside him and Zander at the head of the party, he reveals to me a lure, bait that he uses when hunting to try to draw the beasts of the wild to him to be caught.

He reaches into his pocket and hands me a small flask. I set about opening it up but his hand clamps down and stops me.

"No no, not here, girl."

"What is it?"

"A special potion," he says. "Made from the bodies of the beasts here in the woods. Certain creatures find it impossible to ignore."

"You use it for traps?"

"Yes, we do. And tonight, perhaps it will come in handy…"

We press on, several miles still to travel before we reach the end of the wood. It begins to grow less tangled as we go, the canopy less dense and the trees more spaced out, similar to how they began to disperse up in the hills to the base of the northern mountains. It's less foreboding than the stifling jungle the Bear-Skins live in, the place I like to call the 'Cursed Woods'. Perhaps it's the influence of the Fangs in these parts, the forest seeming to mimic their friendlier demeanour rather than the oppressive woods that went rather well with Bjorn and his brutal troop.

I wonder just what's happening with them. Bjorn and fifty of his men were killed, yes, but surely his tribe is similar in size to the Fangs. It's quite possible that they have hundreds of people living towards the north of Haven too. Maybe the Cure even sent an envoy their way as well?

It's certainly conceivable, though I suspect that their interest in the Fangs lay more in Rhoth's tribes' position here in the west. If they're to pass this way, better to gain the support of the local tribe, especially if they have information that could be useful in sieging the city.

I certainly doubt they expected things to go this way. The envoy was clearly a highly gifted Mind-Manipulator, and capable of influencing even a mind as strong and resolute as Rhoth's. They probably assume he's currently on board, their two hundred or so soldiers set to pour forward and find the Fangs a willing ally in the fight against Haven, the great oppressors.

They won't find that, of course, but will instead be met by a local tribe unintimidated by this incoming horde. And frankly, the fact that Zander was lying about the telepathic link will turn out to be a good thing in more ways than one.

Yes, the Fangs' hunters are useful in swelling our ranks. Yes, it's good that the rest will be taken care of in Haven. But beyond that, the fact that the envoy didn't warn of the Fangs' refusal to join is a very good thing indeed. They might otherwise have known full well that they were stepping towards a forest filled with waiting enemies. Now, our ambush may just do its job.

Maybe...

Zander continues to attempt contact with Beckett, growing increasingly frustrated the longer he goes without a full update. All he seems to manage on the radio is static and broken words, the link distorted and impossible to decipher. The only good sign is that, from the few words we do hear, Beckett's voice comes down the line.

He is, therefore, alive. I'd begun to grow worried that we'd missed the party.

Only when Rhoth joins the conversation does he offer some solution. Or, I should say, some reason as to what might be causing the problem.

"You don't come this way often, do you boy?" he asks Zander.

"Never," says my brother. "Not this far."

"Then you won't know that there's an old base around here. It has a radio tower of some kind. It might be scrambling your signal."

Zander breathes out a sigh of relief.

"Ah, OK...that makes sense. Good. I thought it might be something worse. Where is this tower?"

"Towards the northern edge of the forest near the

base of the mountains. There are lots of ruins of the old world there. I think it was a military base of some sort. We have found weapons there in the past."

"Oh right, so that's where you got your rifles and handguns?" I ask.

The big man nods.

"Some of them, yes. Perhaps, with us being such close allies now, however, we will get some more of your fancy rifles," he says, admiring the pulse rifle he took off Zander weeks ago. "This thing makes a man twice as capable. I would like some more for my hunters."

"There's plenty to spare in the city," I say. "I've literally seen them just lying around in the streets. So many people have died…they don't need them anymore."

Rhoth nods sombrely.

"Your big city is in pain. It is such a shame, all this war. We Fangs prefer peace if we can have it."

"So do we, Rhoth," says Zander. "That's what we're fighting for."

"Yes. And now we fight together again. Are you ready, boy?" he asks, looking at my brother's shoulder, padded and bandaged beneath his gear. "Your wounds have healed?"

"Healing," corrects Zander. "I should be asking you that, Rhoth. You were worse than me after your clash with Bjorn. Speaking of which, we brought medicine for you…"

"Ah, not needed. Just more scars to add to the many others. Superficial wounds, my boy. And the pain...I like to use the pain. Keeps me alert."

"Well, the offer's there. Let's just try to avoid adding any scars tonight, how about that?"

"I agree! Now tell me more of who is awaiting us?"

"Um, about fifty Nameless," says Zander. "And...fifty Stalkers."

"Ah yes, you and your Savant enemy are now working together against a common threat. It's like us, really. We joined to help you against old Director Cromwell...and now he joins us too. I wonder," he chuckles, "whether this army called the Cure will be the next to join our fight against some other menace!"

He laughs heartily to himself, another of Rhoth's jokes that he thoroughly enjoys, even if no one else does.

"I'm sure this is the last alliance," says Zander placidly. "With Cromwell, it's temporary. I trust that our pact, our friendship, will be more enduring?"

"I hope so, boy," says Rhoth, his laughter dying away. "The Fangs and the Nameless are friends as far as I am concerned. And so are we," he adds, looking at my brother, and then to me.

We both smile back.

"Now, on we rush," gallops Rhoth's voice. "I wish to see how these Stalkers fight!"

The speed picks up once more, the light fading quickly now and the moon beginning to glow. With a few more attempts, Zander picks up some extra morsels of information from Beckett, the sparse offerings signalling his position just south of the river that flows from the high passes, cutting diagonally across the plains.

Zander knows enough to be aware of just where that is, the woods bottlenecking somewhat around the waterway, with several larger, hilly areas filled with rocky outcrops littering it on either side. It is, according to Rhoth, the most obvious entry point into the woods from the grasslands, and has plenty of excellent vantage points for lookouts as well as areas where traps can quite easily be laid.

With Beckett's precise location now known, we learn also that the enemy are still yet to arrive. The information is broken, but I think I hear Beckett say something along the lines of, "They'll be here in under an hour."

Zander confirms that that sounds about right, and Rhoth, knowing the woods so well, informs us that we'll be there in good time to get set and lay some traps of our own.

No further words are shared or spoken between us. We clatter forward as quickly as we can, the hundred hunters at our backs hurdling roots and dodging bushes, the clinking of fangs and claws on necklaces joining the rushing feet to set a strange soundtrack to our trip.

Each minute counts now, and everyone knows it.

And soon we're reaching the old ruins of a long dead town, now gobbled up by the forest, the foundations of buildings and old walls joining the trees and shrubbery. We slow, and from the ruins dark figures appear, silhouettes of men and women, of soldiers, on edge and ready to pounce.

"Hold your fire," I hear a voice calling out, as if weapons were preparing to unleash their fury.

Then, from behind an old wall, Beckett rushes forward, looking upon our assembly with a surgical eye.

"Zander, you're here," he says, emerging from the gloom. "What's been going on with your radio?"

"Rhoth says it's an old radio tower north of here. There's a military base or something..."

"Ah, I see, well that explains a lot." He turns to Rhoth. "Good to have you with us, Rhoth. I see you've brought some friends with you..."

"All who can fight have come," growls the big Fang. "We seek revenge on these people who come to kill us."

"Revenge?"

"Long story," says Zander. "All you need to know is we have about a hundred Fangs here, and the rest of them are heading to Haven. There was an envoy in their village trying to get them onside. He, um, failed."

"Good to hear it," grunts Beckett approvingly. "You're a loyal man, Rhoth. But we have plenty of hybrids to deal with the coming threat."

"Perhaps, perhaps not," says Zander. "I got into the envoy's head before he died. Cromwell hasn't been lying to us, Beckett. This army call themselves the Cure. They're barbarians, tearing through the western lands and gathering warriors to their cause. They are no rabble. They will be no pushover. The two hundred sent ahead are going to be much tougher than we thought."

"Hmmmm, ill news," says Beckett pensively. "Any details on what sorts of hybrids are coming?"

"None I'm afraid," says Zander. "Just that we're in for a rough night. Where are Colonel Hatcher and the Stalkers?"

Beckett bends his neck off to the left and the other end of the clearing. The woods are peppered not with old ruins there, but rocks and craggy outcrops, places of cover from which to fight.

"He's set up over there. He's to cover the left flank, us the right. We have set some traps ahead and have Hawks in place to give warning of incoming danger. Rhoth, you know these lands better than we do," says Beckett, giving the big Fang the sort of respect he craves. "Do you see any weak points in our line of defence?"

Rhoth considers it for a time, searching left and right.

"You're well covered here in the ruins, and to the left among the rocks," he says. "My Fangs can take position in ambush spots. We are used to hunting, and know how to stay silent and unseen. We will work in pods and snatch as many lives as we can."

"OK. Take positions. But retreat if you're under heavy attack. I know you're fine hunters, but some warriors you won't be able to contend with."

It's the sort of thing that I suspect might insult Rhoth, but he merely nods and takes it on board. Because, though Rhoth is a proud man and great warrior, he and his Fangs do have their limitations. They will be no match for the more powerful hybrids.

"We'll help where we can," he says. "I have some traps of my own I'd like to set. We have bait that will lure creatures here. They will cause…distraction, if not more."

Beckett nods.

"Good. I trust you to know just what you're doing, Rhoth. We don't want any beasts distracting *us* now do we?"

"Not to worry, Mr Beckett. I'll set the bait on the edge of the forest. If the beasts come, they'll cause problems for the Cure. They may give away their position, or break apart. There's no harm in the attempt."

"Right, do what you need, and do it quick. We have little time before the enemy arrive. Oh, and Rhoth, keep an eye out for our traps. They're mainly down the centre, designed to bottleneck the incoming soldiers. Go left and right to avoid them."

Rhoth nods and hurries off with the Fangs, West to his side. Beckett turns to Zander and me.

"It's good to have you two here," he says. "Take

position within the ruins. Our traps, as I say, are right ahead." He points out the area between the ruins and the rocks, the entry point into the woods from the grasslands beyond. "There are explosive tripwires and mobile gun placements that will trigger when we set them off. We're going to try to funnel as many men down this passage as we can, set off the guns, and then shoot them up like fish in a barrel."

"Right, good plan," whispers Zander. "We need to cut down their numbers as fast as we can and level the playing field. Are the Stalkers all on board with this?"

"You know what they're like. They'll follow any order perfectly. Colonel Hatcher and I came up with this together. He's not so bad, considering…"

"OK, good. Let's hope they're as ferocious with this enemy as they've been with us. Nice to have them on our side for a change."

"Hmmm, shame it's come to this," grumbles Beckett. "But, they'll prove useful tonight I'm sure."

And, in the days to come…I hope.

With the night falling, and the odd cloud passing over the moon above, we move into position and wait.

Another day, another battle.

Another chance to die.

CHAPTER NINE

The silence that pervades the forest is deep and long. Hidden within the ruins of an ancient brick building, with my brother alongside me and Beckett not far away, I wait with a growing tension in my bones for the enemy to arrive.

The Fangs are so quiet and quick in their movements that they quickly set their bait and retreat to ambush positions, moving into trees or hiding in small recesses in the dirt, taking positions to the flanks to catch out anyone who might veer off track when the battle begins.

Though the radio signal between my brother and Beckett was disrupted, the communicator used between Beckett and Colonel Hatcher appears in good working order. It seems that the Stalker scouts ahead are feeding the Colonel information, and he is then passing it onto Beckett. The devices they're using are built into their helmets, allowing easily communication in the field within a limited range.

I watch Beckett for updates, and listen as he whispers along the line, spreading the word to the hybrids of the Nameless, hidden among the remains of this old, vine-covered town. I recognise a number of them, Marler in particular, one of the strike team to help take down the High Tower. Others, I hope, are equally gifted killers and fighters.

Soon, the whispers are heralding the arrival of enemy soldiers.

"Get ready," whispers Beckett. "They're coming fast. It sounds like they're not aware of our presence. Total silence now. No movement."

I set my muscles to stone and peer through a gap in the brick wall. Ahead, through the trees, the grasslands beyond are just about visible. I guide my gaze forward as far as I can, searching for the sight of men moving towards us. For several long minutes, I see nothing. Then, from over the crest of a small rise, silhouettes begin to emerge.

I hold my breath firm in my lungs. Ten come, then another twenty, then dozens more as the group work their way towards the trees. They stop at the edge, the sudden gloom of the forest perhaps making them slightly wary. Those with augmented senses use them, the gathering force taking a short time to survey the path ahead to make sure it's safe.

Then, one of them appears to bend low to the ground. He sets about inspecting a patch of earth, some curious smell attracting his attention. It must be one of Rhoth's lures, though as yet no creature appears to have taken the bait.

A failed attempt, perhaps, but worth a shot. The beasts of the wild must know better than to come calling with such a force assembled. They prefer to sneak and snipe from the bushes, unless vastly outnumbering their opponents…

A sudden flurry of movement dispels the notion.

A growling sound penetrates the silence, and from the brush a beast comes charging. I don't see it at first – I only hear it – but the men of the Cure clearly do. They turn as one to the right, and begin lifting their weapons. For the first time I see them – rifles, old and worn like those of the Fangs, knives and other blades, scavenged from the old world.

But not all of them need weapons.

As the men get ready to fire at whatever beast must be coming at them, one of them steps ahead. I watch closely, my eyes zoomed in a hundred or so metres away, and see that it's a gigantic bear that's rushing, frothing at the mouth and turned wild by the scent of whatever Rhoth set to the earth.

The man seems completely unfazed by the charging beast. As it bounds forwards on powerful legs, and the other men stand back with weapons aloft, the man merely holds up one hand, palm facing out at the great monster.

The bear stops abruptly in its tracks, as if suddenly paralysed, its front legs suspended in the air and back legs pressing in the mud. The man raises his hand, and the bear goes too, its body rising up into the air, locked in the same position and unable to move.

Higher and higher it goes, towards the tops of the trees, before the man casually throws his hand off to the left, and the bear goes flying away across the plains. It lands with a crunch of broken legs, tumbling off into the grass and groaning loudly. The men just laugh.

My fingers tighten on my gun as I watch the display. This man is another Elemental, a Mind-Mover. Just like the fire-manipulator I saw in West's memories. Or the wind-manipulator who set that tornado to the streets when those strange soldiers came to take Kira.

I look to my brother and Beckett. Both of them have seen the same as me. Our commander whispers as quietly as he can into his mic – "Note – Elemental spotted. Priority target."

He must be telling Colonel Hatcher. It's such an odd feeling, wishing to see the Stalkers unleashed. I wish them to pour through the woods and destroy these men. To see them do what they were bred for.

But not yet. Still, no one moves, and we lie in wait for the enemy to get closer. For some time they enter into a further discussion, whispers trickling through the trees. I look again at Beckett, his Bat powers enabling him to decipher the conversation. He turns to the men around us and offers a few hand signals and gestures. Zander watches, understands, and then looks to me.

And in my head I hear his voice.

They're suspicious, he tells me. *They suspect a trap. Be ready to fire when Beckett activates the gun placements.*

I nod my understanding, and turn my eyes back to the men. Though wary, they have little choice but to enter through this gateway into the woods. Creeping forward, they come, weapons up and ready, eyes searching high and low.

Then, more growling sounds lift from the edges of the wood, Rhoth's lures once more working their magic. This time, the distraction comes from various angles, the red eyes of the mutated wolves lighting in the darkness. Some men turn to face them, and fire off shots. Others quickly press forward, moving further from the plains.

They begin to disperse, the wolves here undeterred by their weapons and fast enough to creep around mostly unseen. My mind flashes with my own experience of the beasts, Zander once saving Adryan and me from a desperate and gruesome end not so long ago.

These wolves, I know, are not normal. Large and crazed, they have no fear of guns or man. They move fast and have thick hides, their bodies growing natural defences against the harsh features of this land. And these men of the Cure, I suspect, won't have had dealings with such beasts before.

And as with the Stalkers, now our temporary allies in this fight, the creatures of the wood join us too in defending their lands, as if aware of just what threat these men pose.

They come from both sides, drawn here from afar and made mad by the scent of blood. The woods begin to light with the flame of gunfire, the men now moving quickly towards our position in the ruins, entering the bottleneck where we'll strike them down.

Several rush a little quicker, those tasked with inspecting the path ahead distracted by the sudden attack. They enter into our world, and their nostrils suck up the poison that infects our lands. It will affect some of them, dull their senses and powers, their bodies unused to these strange conditions. And rushing on, those at the front fail to see that death is looming.

They clatter through the brush, and I see one catch his leg on a tripwire. The explosion that follows is enough to consume him and half a dozen men around him, splitting limbs from bodies and setting flesh aflame. The blast is the catalyst for the carnage that follows. Men begin to dart in all directions, seeking their enemy, and more of them hit the traps hidden in the undergrowth.

Explosions begin to light up the woods to the left and right of the clearing, forcing the rest of the men to charge straight forward. With fire to their flanks and wolves at their backs, they pour further inland, right to where we wait.

Then gunfire, rapid and unceasing, fills the air too. Several hidden guns, fixed into the earth or up in the trees, begin to spew down upon our enemy. They rattle ferociously, and I see more men fall, too slow to react. Many, however, are fast enough. They dash off left and right, or spread further forward, and come right into the path of our waiting men.

It's time for us to join. And Beckett is the first to fire.

Standing, he launches the red blaze of his pulse

rifle into the fray, and a second later fifty hybrids of the Nameless, and another fifty Stalkers are doing the same. All across this small stretch of woodland, leading towards the vast forest beyond, the world lights with a mixture of red, green, and blue flame; a beautiful but deadly display.

The men of the Cure take little time to fire back. Launching themselves into positions they can defend, or retreating a little further back to the plains, they set about peppering our positions with barrages of their own.

The wall I hide behind immediately draws fire. It spits and cracks and chips away at the brick, the ruins of the old town taking further damage. Crouching right next to my brother, I mimic his movements as he fires over the wall and ducks away from incoming fire, his eyes and mine just about able to see the fizzing yellow trails of the incoming bullets as they light up in the dark night.

It's impossible for me to know just how many men have fallen within the enemy ranks. Yet the ambush played out well, the traps doing their part and the funnel working to catch the enemy within a world of pain. Now, however, the fight looks set to break apart, men using the considerable gifts they have to turn their own personal battles to their advantage.

What becomes clear is that they're mostly Dashers, or more likely hybrids with Dasher blood. Both sides are filled with them, confirming what I've always thought – a warrior isn't much of a warrior unless they have superior speed. Few other enhancements are as useful in battle, and clearly the Cure are well aware of that.

So, the bottleneck we caught them in quickly clears out. They rush in various directions, sweeping though the woods and engaging where they can, or moving backwards where they can try to regroup. The wolves behind suddenly become of secondary concern, and many of them scramble off into the trees, realising that this fight isn't for them any longer.

When it's done, they'll have plenty of flesh to feed on. No need for them to lose their lives now.

Within the madness, I try to pick out the Elemental, but find it impossible. All I can do is fire into the maelstrom and hope I hit some targets, ducking low whenever any bullets try to hunt me down. Before long, however, our wall is disintegrating, large chunks chipped away and no longer suitable for cover.

"Displace!" I hear my brother call.

He rushes to me, grabs my arm, and begins dragging me off further back into the ruins. We dive behind more cover, and I see that Beckett remains where he was, right there on the front line, firing his red flame at anyone who comes near.

Across the way, the Stalkers shift here and there, black shapes moving between the trees. I get the odd flash of close quarter combat, some of the Cure having rushed off to the left and engaging the Stalkers head on. I have no time to watch or dwell. I only have time to shoot and hide, the battle unlike any other I've yet been in, more relentless and ferocious.

Soon, the woods are flaming all over, set to blaze by the blasts from the traps and the rounds of pulse energy spewing from a hundred guns. It lights the world up, but the smoke makes visibility poor. Before too long, I'm firing only at shapes in the murk, or at the tips of firing rifles as they give away enemy positions.

The fire, however, is set to work in our enemy's favour. I see it churning and gathering in an unnatural formation, before pouring forward as if sent from some giant flame-thrower. I know, immediately, that a fire-manipulator is here, and perhaps more than one. Could it be that the man who helped destroy West's village is among them? Could he be the man now sending the licking tongues of flame right at us?

I have no time to consider the question. The fire comes calling, spreading violently through the ruins of the old town; down old streets and between the broken, dirty windows of old cars. The orange and yellow tendrils stretch out, gripping at whatever they can take hold of, and old walls and crumbling foundations, covered in green vines and creepers, begin to burn and melt.

Some men, too slow to see or react, or otherwise caught with their attention elsewhere, get eaten up by the murderous blaze. I watch in horror as the bodies of several Nameless are consumed, dropping to the floor and trying in vain to roll and smother the flames. It's no use. Within mere seconds, they're still. Dead. The fire too hot to contend with for long.

I'm forced to retreat once more, Zander calling for others to do the same. I look left, and see more fire spreading in the direction of the Stalkers. It hunts them down, gobbling them up along with any men of the Cure caught with them in combat. And as the flames gallop, I see a shape in the smoke, swirling his hands, calling down a ferocious wind that serves to press the fire further into the woods.

Rushing away, I feel the smoke pouring into my lungs through heaving breaths. I cough it up, dragging my mask – which I'd discarded – back up over my mouth. Others are moving back too, the pelt and fur covered figures of the Fangs realising they can do no more. Perhaps they've killed some who fell into their little ambushes. Perhaps not.

Perhaps many of them have lost their lives too, drawn to this battle and, as I feared, too out of their depth to fight such men.

Yet it is the Elementals who have changed things. The combination of fire and strong winds now buffet us, still following as we withdraw. What started as us displacing to escape the blaze has turned into a full retreat. I hear my brother roaring over the din, "Move back! Get away from the fire!"

The Nameless around us who are still alive, and who are able to hear him, take note. Not all, however, are in that boat. Some still lie hidden from the flames, surrounded and unable to move, their paths away from the battle cut off by the heat. I see one, and through the thick smoke realise that it's

Beckett, eyes searching left, right, forward and backwards for a way to flee.

I grab Zander's arm to stop him.

"Beckett!" I shout. "He's caught!"

My brother's fierce hazel eyes, lit by the fire, quickly find Beckett too, still within the ruins and unable to get out. I see the dilemma play out in his mind, see him looking for a way to help.

He seems to make a snap call, the sort driven by the desire to save a friend, and begins rushing back towards the fray.

He doesn't get far.

In a horrible moment, as Beckett turns and sees Zander coming, I watch as he lifts his hand and shakes his head, shouting out, "NO! STOP!"

He knows there's no way out for him. He knows Zander is merely rushing to his own death. So, lifting his handgun to his temple, he makes one final plea.

"GET THEM OUT. RETREAT TO THE CITY!" he calls.

Then, before Zander can move any further, Beckett sends a bullet through his own brain.

CHAPTER TEN

I rush straight for my brother as he stands there, motionless. I grab his arm and pull back. He doesn't shift for a second.

"Zander!" I shout. "We have to go!"

Over the roaring flames and wind, my words get through. He escapes his short paralysis and turns, Beckett's body now hidden on the ground and covered in flame.

We begin moving east away from the ruins, and ahead I see the shapes of the Nameless escaping too. On the other side, the Stalkers do the same. They slip from cover to cover, unable to withstand the fire that now blocks off all visibility ahead.

The hunters are now the hunted, chased off into the woods by a wall of fire that consumes all before it. I have no time or opportunity to search for the Fangs, my eyes set only on the cool air of the woodland ahead as we dash for cover and escape the chasing inferno.

I can feel the terrible heat at my back, the storm of fire spreading wildly through the woods. Yet our Dasher powers are enough to give us some space, and soon we're able to stop and turn and witness the carnage behind.

The forest is burning from left to right. By now a dozen acres must be wreathed in flame, and each second more ground is covered. Smoke fills the sky, black and thick and suffocating, spreading all through the trees and making it impossible to catch sight of our allies, or work out just how many are still alive.

Over the roar, Zander once more calls out for all to retreat to Haven. I see a few shapes tearing away, fearing for their lives. They're quickly taken by the smoke and disappear, leaving me with only Zander.

"Rhoth…" I say. "West…"

He stops me short.

"They know what to do, Brie," he tells me. "We can't look for them. We can't wait for them. We have no choice but to withdraw."

We continue on again, stretching off from the flames and rushing through the smoke. Jutting roots and fallen trees hinder us, unseen until the last moment. I trip on one and tumble, the air pressed from my lungs. Zander quickly hauls me to my feet and we set off again at a gallop.

As we begin to escape the smoke, my burning lungs call for me to remove my mask. I take it off and suck in several long breaths as we enter into a patch of clearer air, panting hard.

Suddenly, gunshots sound nearby. We swing our eyes and find a collection of enemy soldiers rushing in our direction. The bullets rip at our feet and the trees to our sides as we move off again, hurtling through the thick scrub of the forest floor with the men in hot pursuit.

We reach a clearing with rocks to the left and slide in behind them. Zander snatches a grenade from his belt, flicks a switch, and tosses it back in the direction we came. Seconds later, the men are rushing through and passing straight by it, setting it off by proximity. Zander throws his body over me as the explosion rips through the clearing, tearing the men apart and battering the rocks with debris.

The rain of dust and blood that follows coats the glade in red and black. We step from our cover and confirm that our pursuers are dead, before setting back off once more.

Four more to add to the departed. Four less to siege the city in the days to come.

For the next five minutes, Zander leads me on, our enhanced speed quickly taking us away from the battle. Only when my reserves of energy begin to fade do we slow and rest for a second. I fall to the base of a tree, head in my hands and chest heaving. Zander stays on his feet, fit as a fiddle, eyes scanning behind to ensure we're alone.

We are.

But in the distance, the devastation remains clear. The world lights in a cocktail of colour: yellow and orange and red below, black above as the fire breathes thick smoke into the night sky. The enemy army, still many miles away, will be able to see it from the grasslands, rushing perhaps to join. Maybe all we've done this night is precipitate the attack on the city. Maybe we've just enraged the beast.

But on we press. We have to, and have no choice now but to navigate our way back east and hope as many of our people got out alive as possible. The city, miles away, will take hours to reach at regular pace, and with the night falling and woods growing quiet, we know the threat of the wilds will grow prominent again.

Such is the way here when the sun falls. No night is safe no matter who you are. After some time, we decide to stop again, knowing now that we've lost anyone who might be chasing.

"They'll be gathering again," Zander tells me with conviction. "They came to carve a path through the woods to Haven. So that's what they'll be doing."

What none of us had thought, however, was that they'd use fire to do it. It may just be that they had plans to burn down the forest regardless as to whether we attacked them en route or not. Still, far away, it's obvious that the flames are being fanned, the Elementals pressing them forward and melting the woods, charring the earth and making it easy for a force of thousands to pass through.

The beasts will be forced to retreat as we are, and the Shadows that lurk will seek other grounds. The village of the Fangs will be caught up in it too, dozens of square miles worth of woodland razed to the ground, the earth scorched as if mimicking the more arid lands these people seem to hail from.

So, though I wish to rest and stop in some secret crevice until dawn, we cannot risk such a thing. The constant rush of my life continues, and we spend hour on hour on the march, only stopping intermittently to snatch brief periods of rest.

We pass no one and see no one. Only Zander, experienced tracker as he is, spots the occasional track in the mud that speaks of one of our allies heading east.

He stops to inspect them but only briefly, identifying the type of footwear on show. There appears to be a mixture, the boots worn by the Nameless all coming in different shapes and sizes, those of the Stalkers all identical. From the direction of travel, it appears as though the surviving Stalkers are making their way back to the REEF, with the Nameless heading for the western gate to Outer Haven. No tracks are discovered to identify the Fangs.

"Don't worry," Zander tells me, equally adept at identifying my emotional state as searching for tracks. "Rhoth will lead his people to safety. They'll be fine, Brie."

I have to take his word for it.

As we get closer to the city, he starts to attempt contact with the gate using the radio. At first we appear out of range, but soon enough he's able to get through, hastily informing the garrison to expect our forces to arrive in dribs and drabs.

None, by the sounds of it, have yet arrived. That's no surprise given how we're still many miles out. However, he does learn that the Fangs from the village have made it safely, and have been transferred to a nearby camp within the city walls. I just have to hope that most of their hunters manage to return to join them.

The night goes on, and through the thickening canopy in the heart of the forest, the light of the moon and stars is further blotted. I find my ability to see in the dark somewhat muted here, owing to my ever-increasing state of exhaustion. My Dasher powers are all but depleted, my energy reserves now low enough to force us to do little more than walk at a brisk pace.

All the while, Zander's own reserves remain rather more full. Over the many years he's had utilising and evolving his powers, he's grown capable of maintaining them for far longer in combat and under physical duress. Right now, I'm little better than a regular Unenhanced, my physical capabilities having reached their limit and my body in dire need of rest to rebuild and recuperate my energy stores.

Zander, however, knows his limits far better, and I'm well aware that they're far deeper than my own. I can operate in small bursts mostly, and when using my Dasher powers, my fitness continues to be a problem. Without him here right now, I'd be extremely vulnerable here in the wilds. And even with him, we remain in a dangerous situation so far from home.

As I continue to flag and slow, Zander takes the decision to head for the REEF. At any other time, it would appear to be folly to choose such a course. But times being as they are, he assures me it's a sensible move.

"The Stalkers will be arriving soon, if not already," he says. "Cromwell will no doubt be readying himself and his people to move for the city. It won't take long for the Cure's army to spread this way, and seeing as they're burning down the forest, Cromwell can't wait at the REEF any longer in case the flames spread this way."

I know he's right, although I'm sure the REEF wouldn't be affected by the burning forest. Its walls are high and thick and the tree line ends a decent distance from them, giving them a nature buffer. Yet, the risk isn't the flames, but what will come after them.

"So…we hitch a ride?" I ask.

"Exactly. We're still a long way from the western gate. It sounds odd to say it, I know, but we'll be safer travelling with Director Cromwell and the Stalkers."

Odd indeed. But, right now I have no strength to quibble.

"Fine. If you think it's best," I say.

With the REEF not too far away, we begin diverting our course, travelling slightly to the south rather than heading directly east. By now, the mountains are growing larger to the north, and were it still standing, the High Tower might just be visible in the distance too.

Alas, that beacon has gone, and now here we are, facing a rampaging horde. I can't deny that it grates quite deeply, knowing that Cromwell hasn't lied to us once. Knowing that everything he's said has been accurate. And that we do now rely very heavily on his Stalkers in order to help keep the city safe.

I think, in many ways, I wished to find some deceit in him. I wished that he'd been tricking us all along, merely using all of this as a means of creeping his way back through the door and reinstating himself within the ranks of the city. I wished for it, in the end, so it would give me a better opportunity to seek my vengeance when he was found out.

Yet, perhaps that won't happen. Maybe we really do need him…need each other.

With the night beginning to lighten just a touch, and the first threads of dawn not too far away, the wall of the REEF comes into view. I shudder at the sight of it, this place of suffering and pain and torture. A place where normal people are made into slaves, or terminated for not fitting in with my grandfather's vision of the world.

It is an evil, cold, oppressive place, and within it right now, so many people who share its characteristics reside. Our long time enemy, turned temporary ally. And, who knows, perhaps our ties might just tighten in the times to come.

I hate the idea, of course, and so many others will too. Yet I have no authority within this arrangement to determine our course. I have no choice but to leave that up to better minds than mine. And, above all, I trust my grandmother to do what's best for the people under her care. As much as I hate my grandfather, she has far more claim to that than I. And if she can form a partnership for our mutual benefit, who exactly am I to argue against it?

So, as I look upon the REEF, and feel that horrible shudder run up my spine, I keep my thoughts to myself. I walk beside my brother, who also has more claim than I do to detest having to come here, who's spent his life fighting these people and what they represent, and make my way towards the front gate.

And inside, the rumbling of engines filters through their air, and the shuffling of movement sounds. Atop the walls, some of the City Guards stationed here see us coming. They call out for us to halt, and we do so immediately.

Arms aloft, Zander shouts out for them not to shoot. In such times, they may have orders to shoot on the spot anyone not garbed as either City Guards or Stalkers.

"My name is Zander, commander of the forces of the Nameless," my brother calls out. "We have come from the battle at the edge of the woods. We fight with the Stalkers, and with Director Cromwell, and we require transfer to Haven immediately…"

The men instantly recognise him, and their weapons are quickly lowered. The gates begin to grind open, and through we pass into the REEF.

Not as captives, but friends.

CHAPTER ELEVEN

The main square within the REEF is bustling and busy. Stalkers and City Guards march around here and there. A large convoy of vehicles is being prepared to move out, the REEF emptied and all personnel transferred to the safety of Haven.

Arriving inside, we find a stern looking man walking our way, his black armour showing signs of recent battle. His face is craggy, eyes severe and dark, probably in his early forties by the looks of him. I know immediately that this is the leader of the Stalkers, Colonel Hatcher.

"Zander," he says, marching straight for my brother. "We haven't officially met, but I know just who you are. I see you managed to escape the fight. I'm not surprised."

"Nor am I to see you here, Colonel Hatcher. How many of your Stalkers made it out?"

"Most," he says gruffly. "Not all have been accounted for yet. Some got separated during the battle. They may be dead or merely yet to return. About thirty-five are here. We may have lost ten or more."

He speaks without any apparent caring for the men he's lost. That isn't surprising at all. Yet, as Lady

Orlando said, he does remind me of Beckett, so recently departed. I guess now that he's gone, my brother is the rebels' most senior military officer.

Then again, can we still call ourselves rebels? It doesn't seem appropriate anymore…

"That's a heavy loss," says Zander, seeming rather more concerned by it than Hatcher. "I don't yet know how many Nameless were killed…"

"And Commander Beckett?" questions Hatcher.

"Dead," says Zander, shaking his head. "He got caught in the flames. Ordered the retreat, then…" He trails off, refusing to finish the sentence.

"A shame," says Colonel Hatcher. "We can ill afford to lose men with the capabilities of Commander Beckett." He looks at me for the first time. "I see this is your sister, Brie. You look weary, young lady. I imagine you came here to seek transfer to Haven?"

"Yes," says Zander. "The path through the woods is dangerous. We thought it best to travel with the convoy, assuming you're leaving soon?"

"We are. Director Cromwell has been in communication with Lady Orlando. She has green-lit our transfer to Outer Haven. We can't afford to stay here much longer with this enemy approaching."

"The Cure," says Zander. "That's what they call themselves. Were you not aware of their strength, Colonel? Surely your intel informed you that they'd have Elementals with them?"

"We had some knowledge of what sorts of soldiers they possessed," he admits calmly. "Yet we couldn't have known about their true capabilities. We wouldn't have chosen to willingly walk into such a battle if we had, would we?"

"Perhaps not. Clearly they took us all by surprise. Where's Director Cromwell?"

"Inside. We'll be moving momentarily. This way, follow me."

He leads us through the main square and sea of bodies, ripping like black and grey waves as they go about their duties. The various buildings of the REEF, tall and intimidating with harsh, uninviting facades, sit ahead. We enter into the central building and move down the featureless corridor into an office. There, we find a reception committee I'd prefer to never have to deal with.

The white clad remains of the Consortium, Agent Woolf, and Director Cromwell, all stand around a table. By the looks of things, they're discussing the night's events and imminent transfer to Haven. All look more dishevelled than ever, their once pristine clothing growing dirtier by the day. It's as if all their suits and special Consortium attire was blown up along with the High Tower, leaving them with the unpalatable option of either wearing something below their station, or merely sticking with their current clothing and letting themselves fester.

Colonel Hatcher is the first to speak.

"Apologies for the interruption, Director Cromwell. We have special guests."

He steps aside to reveal Zander and me. All eyes turn to us with little to no surprise within them.

"Ah, I see. Thank you, Colonel Hatcher. Please continue to make preparations for the convoy."

"Yes, Director," says Hatcher, before slipping from the room.

Standing there, I feel rather vulnerable, as if I've just willingly stepped into a nest of venomous snakes. Yet, the reality is quite different – after all, it's my brother and me who are armed to the teeth. Should we wish it, we could wipe out the entire top brass of the old enemy right now.

It's a real sign of the times that the thought comes and goes with so little conviction. It would, of course, mean both of our deaths. And, well, we can't exactly kill Cromwell knowing how his Stalkers and Con-Cops will react. But still, even without those conditions, the temptation to kill the lot of them, which would once have been so strong, isn't currently present.

Right now, there's a much bigger threat facing the city that we have to deal with together.

"Zander and Brie, a pleasure to welcome you here under better circumstances than the last time," says Cromwell. "I'm happy to see you survived the battle without too much ill effect. I understand you don't yet know how many of your men survived?"

"Not yet, Director Cromwell," says Zander. "I hope no worse a ratio than your Stalkers."

"I hope so too. It appears we were a little

underprepared for what came our way."

"Yes," says Zander swiftly. "At least now we know just what we're facing. You were correct on numbers. There's at least ten thousand in the main army."

Cromwell nods.

"And where did you get this confirmation?"

"An envoy was sent to the Fangs. I discovered the information from him. They are barbarians who call themselves the Cure. They are more of a plague, Director. They spread through the lands and take what people and resources they can. They have been building up to this for years. Destroying Haven is their ultimate goal."

"Yes indeed, I am aware," says Cromwell calmly. "I did tell you all this already. Naturally, your trust in me is somewhat lacking. I understand and appreciate that. However, perhaps now what information I give you all will be taken at face value?"

"I'd imagine so," says Zander.

"Good. I have my intel, yet it isn't enough to build a complete picture of these people. What you have witnessed tonight is worrying, very worrying indeed. We can only hope that the main force isn't as capable as those you faced this evening."

"They won't be," asserts Zander confidently. "We were undone by fire tonight. We can't let that happen again. Had their Elementals not been present, we'd have defeated them, of that I'm sure.

We have to make those men the absolute priority targets. Fighting against a wall of flame is impossible, Director. If they breach the city walls, there's no reason why they won't be able to turn Haven into an inferno."

"Yes, Colonel Hatcher thought along similar lines, young man. I suggest you work closely with him from this point on."

Zander nods.

"I will do what is necessary to protect the city and the people," he says proudly.

"Indeed. And so our alliance deepens through death. You will both ride with me to Haven. It will be a nice signal to the city that our paths are now entwined."

I clench my teeth weakly at the suggestion. If I had more energy my jaw would clamp tighter.

"Right then, there's little point in delaying further," continues Cromwell. He looks to his companions, and gestures for them to gather up their things. "Everyone, head outside. We will further our talks back in the city…"

As they begin to prepare for departure, I start to wonder just who else might still be here. The REEF, after all, is a place used for extermination and reconditioning, and has cells filled with mostly innocent people awaiting that fate. Are those cells full right now?

As the Consortium begin moving out through the door, I speak for the first time.

"I trust the cells here are empty, Director," I say.

He turns to me, but doesn't answer immediately.

Then he smiles.

"Brie, ever the moral crusader. I can see what you're getting at."

"So, are they?" I ask again.

He shakes his head.

"They are not empty, I'm afraid to say."

"Then make sure they are," I say immediately. "What were you planning to do? Leave people in their cells to die?"

"It sounds callous to you, of course," says Cromwell. "However, these people were only going to be terminated anyway, or else reconditioned and made to serve. With time being so short, we have no opportunity to do that now…"

"Jeez. Stop and listen to yourself. At least you admit it sounds callous. Let them out immediately!"

Cromwell draws back and straightens up, unused to being talked to in such a fashion. Those still in the room look to him to see how he might react. I feel no compulsion to tiptoe around this despot. He needs someone to set his moral compass to order, an impossible task though it is.

"We don't have the space to take them back to the city," he says. "These people are criminals under the laws of Haven…"

"*Criminals*!" I say, ready to put him straight on

that matter. He shuts me down before I can get going.

"BUT…" he says loudly, halting my voice. "I will concede that at times of war, exceptions can be made. "I will be prepared to release the prisoners and let them make their way to the city on foot…"

"Nope, not good enough, Artemis," I say, my use of his first name deliberately disrespectful. *If I can't kill him, I'll damn well disrespect him whenever possible.* "It's too dangerous on the road. We'll head for Haven and send the convoy back to collect them."

"Brie," mutters Cromwell, trying to hide his anger. "What makes you think you have any authority to make demands here?"

"Me? Well, sure, I don't have much. But get Lady Orlando on the line, and you'll get your authority. I'm fairly sure she'll side with *me*, Artemis, and not *you*. Don't trip yourself up here. Just do it, OK. Do a good thing for once in your damn life."

My continued disrespect draws Zander's voice into my head. I hear him whispering for me to cool my tongue and stop aggravating him.

I can't. I'm having too much of a good time seeing the expression on his otherwise placid face. Oh, how he tries to hide it. It's bloody well hilarious seeing him losing even a modicum of his perpetual cool.

For several moments, he considers it. Then, seeing that I've got him pretty well cornered, concedes. It's a small victory for me, and goes some small way to satisfying my lust for vengeance against the man.

"Fine, have it your way, Brie. I'll order the convoy returned here to release the prisoners once we're safely at Haven. And if you're so very keen on seeing them safe, perhaps you'd like to go with them?"

"Happy to…" I begin, rising to the challenge.

This time, Zander steps in.

"No, not wise," he says quickly. "Brie needs her rest for the battles to come."

I look at my brother, unhappy to be talked for. Again, his voice filters through my mind.

Stop it, Brie! he says. *You've won. Leave it at that.*

Fine, I say back, without admitting that I'm about ready to collapse from total exhaustion.

With my victory assured, we all move back out of the building and into the night. The first light of dawn is now on the march, the sky growing a little brighter and set to beckon a sunny new day. Yet so far from here, on the edge of the forest, I know the fires will still be raging, and the woods that call home to many people and creatures burning to the ground.

And beyond, the army of the Cure will be marching, still trekking across the wide plains. The orange glow will stretch out before them, creating the vast path of charred earth upon which they will travel. It is an omen of death, a black, lifeless road that will stretch for miles towards their final goal.

And when they come, several days from now, we have to be ready. Because if we fail, all men, women, and children within the city will perish. And our war between the Consortium and the Nameless, our fight for the future, won't include either of us.

That future will belong to someone else entirely.

CHAPTER TWELVE

The journey back to Haven doesn't take long, but the time is does take is spent rather uncomfortably. Not uncomfortable in a physical sense so much as a mental one. Having to sit beside Agent Romelia Woolf and opposite Director Cromwell is the sort of travel arrangement that nightmares are made of.

Along with Zander, the four of us sit in the rear of a car in the midst of the convoy of City Guards and Stalkers, a powerful grouping of soldiers if ever there was one. I find Woolf looking at me as we go, seemingly never-ending in her attempts to infiltrate my mind and discover my innermost thoughts.

In the end, her constant staring breaks me. I look right at her, thinking that I'd love to smack that smugness right from her ugly face. She sees the thought play out in my mind and merely lifts her horrible smirk a little higher.

"Stop. Staring," I growl at her, finding my weariness constantly pressed to one side by my anger among these people.

She doesn't. She continues to look at me, her expression completely flat but for the little curls in the corners of her mouth.

It's so aggravating that I'm unable to help myself.

The only thing that stops me from making good on my threat is Zander's speed, his fingers quick enough to reach out and grab my wrist before my fist hunts down Woolf's nose with the aim of permanently rearranging it.

"Now now, Romelia, stop antagonising our guest," says Cromwell. "We're all friends here now."

And there it is again, that word that really doesn't describe us at all. I can't tell whether he does it just to piss me off, but it really does serve that purpose as much as Woolf's staring black eyes.

I sit back and heave a breath into my lungs, and turn away from them both. Yet still, I can feel Woolf's eyes on me even now.

The journey seems to last forever. Once again, I hear Zander providing some calming words in my head, but sometimes they do little more than annoy me rather than effectively placate me. I guess right now I'm just too tired to take any of this bullshit. Tired after battle, sick of seeing death, and worried that my friends among the Fangs have met their unnecessary ends.

It's a cocktail that makes me unsuitable for public consumption right now. I need a quiet space to myself where I can sleep and recharge and try to set myself back in order.

This damn car is quite the opposite, sat here with the two people I want dead most in this world.

For the remainder of the journey, I stay quiet and

merely look out of the thick glass window, refusing to re-engage. Meanwhile, Zander continues to operate his radio, getting updates from the city, while occasionally engaging in conversation with Cromwell. I marvel at his ability to put aside his anger and hatred and get on with the job. I guess that's what he's all about right now. It's a skill I've yet to master and one, perhaps, I don't want to.

Still, I'm fully aware that he detests the both of them just as much as I do. I mean, he's been fighting all his life against Cromwell, and though he doesn't yet know the truth of our lineage, Cromwell's constant attempts to kill off the Nameless are plenty to engender a very serious dislike for the man.

And Woolf? Well, he didn't have the same experience as I did with her, haunting my steps in the High Tower, trying to get Adryan to kill me, scuppering my assassination attempt at the final hurdle. However, just as with everyone else, he's fully aware that she's been a real thorn in our side all along, not only informing Cromwell of my aforementioned assassination plot, but also escaping our clutches at the church and getting back to the city just in time to warn of the destruction of the High Tower too. Really, if it wasn't for her, Cromwell and all the rest of them would be dead.

Then again, in some strange twist, perhaps it's good he managed to survive. OK, so it pains me greatly to even think that, but right now I can't deny that it's true. If he was dead, his Stalkers might well be running amok, and so would his Con-Cops, all of them causing havoc within the city. And then this army would arrive to finish us off. Without my grandfather's help, it's highly unlikely the city would survive.

And even now, that hangs in the balance.

I sit and muse on such things as the car rumbles along the dirt track, my mind busy enough to distract me from my companions as I gaze blankly out the window. Before long, the clearing that calls and end to the woods is appearing, and the grand city walls are coming into view.

The western gate sits open, ready to greet us, and several hundred soldiers appear to be gathered at the garrison and atop the walls. I imagine that this side of the city is most at risk of attack, and though we'll have soldiers stationed elsewhere, the west will see the largest contingent.

The convoy quickly flows through the gate, and I finally decide to look at my grandfather's face once again as we pass the threshold. There's a hint of a smile there, some expression of victory. He's back in Outer Haven along with his Stalkers. Yes, there's a large threat heading our way, but in my mind we've just invited another enemy right through the door.

The convoy pulls to a stop, and the Stalkers and City Guards from the REEF spill out. Around us, the eyes of the soldiers of the Nameless appear particularly suspicious of this new alliance, just as mine are. I'm happy to see so many eyes mimicking my own. It makes me feel more secure knowing that there'll be plenty of others keeping an eye on my grandfather and his men.

As Colonel Hatcher sets about arranging the Stalkers, I reiterate to Cromwell that the convoy needs to be sent back out.

"Don't forget the prisoners," I say. "Or do I have to tell Lady Orlando on you?"

He ignores me, and merely waves a hand to one of his minions to see it done. Sure enough, the convoy is quickly heading back to the west, just as my grandmother appears from her own vehicle from the east.

She steps out along with Adryan, and I find myself moving straight for the comfort of his embrace.

"Are you OK?" he whispers softly, eyes equally tender and full of worry.

"I'm fine," I croak, feeling suddenly like I need to be alone with him. Like a few nights ago, where I slept in his arms, and he shielded me from my demons. I need that now. I need him.

Lady Orlando is next to ask me the very same question. I nod again but don't speak this time, feeling suddenly weak and emotionally fragile, as if my voice will break fully if set free.

She cups my cheek all too briefly, a moment of tenderness in full display of Cromwell and Woolf. It's unusual for her to act as such without privacy.

Then she turns to her ex husband.

"Right, Artemis. We'll get you and your people

set up here in the western quarter. There are some nice comfortable tenement blocks that haven't seen too much damage from the fighting. Your men and ours must liaise closely now. As you know, Rycard has been managing the City Guard, and will continue to do so under the leadership of Commander Burns…"

"That makes perfect sense," says Cromwell. "No one knows the City Guard quite like Leyton Burns. Except me, of course. I'll have Colonel Hatcher work closely with the both of them. It's a terrible shame that Mr Beckett was killed tonight."

"A terrible shame," repeats Lady Orlando solemnly. "Zander will now operate at the head of our hybrids."

She looks to my brother, who nods, his young shoulders carrying such a burden.

"I will try to do Beckett proud," he says.

"You will," says Lady Orlando, smiling at her secret grandson. "Any news of Rhoth yet?"

"Nothing," says Zander. "I have faith that he'll come…"

"I wouldn't waste your energy thinking about a tribesman with no enhancements," comes Cromwell's voice. "Yes, these Fangs are fine warriors in the woods, but here in the city their skills count for very little. They are not used to urban warfare. It matters not if this Rhoth returns…"

"It does matter to *us*," counters Lady Orlando

harshly. "Life matters, Artemis, whether it is *useful* to you or not. She turns again to Zander and me, sidestepping Cromwell's heartlessness. "The rest of the Fangs arrived safely some time ago. They are in the southern quarter being tended to by Rycard's wife and several others."

I smile at the thought of Sophie seeing to such people. Perhaps they're even staying at her training house for girls seeking to marry up into Inner Haven. Such a concept seems stupid now. We have all been reduced to the foundational instinct of all living things – to survive. Nothing else matters anymore.

"Are they safe there?" I find myself asking. "Shouldn't they be in Inner Haven behind the wall?"

"They were reticent enough to come into Outer Haven," my grandmother says. "They're safe where they are for now. If needs be, they can be transported further in."

"All very fascinating, Cornelia," cuts in Cromwell. "As I say, wasting your effort tending to such people isn't where your priorities should lie. All current efforts should be focused entirely on destroying this horde who call themselves the Cure."

"Artemis, you run your Stalkers however you want. But I will see that all people in this city are safe. After all, they're the ones we're trying to save."

"Not a bunch of tribespeople we're not."

Lady Orlando holds up her palm, lets a long second of silence fill the air, and then speaks.

"I'm not discussing this with you. Your opinion counts for nothing here. We are allies in one thing, and one thing alone – defending this city. How I like to run it beyond that is nothing to do with you. And yes, before you say otherwise, it is me who is running this city, Artemis. You had your shot and did a god-awful job. Now it's our turn…"

"Oh contraire, Cornelia. The city flourished under my guidance."

"The city, perhaps. But not the people…" she says, before shaking her head to herself. "No, this isn't a debate I'm having with you. As you say, we need a solitary focus right now. So when we speak, we will do so only about defending the city. Now, with that in mind, it's time you set your Con-Cops to do something more useful than sit in the eastern factories and warehouses. They are wasted there, Artemis. There are thousands of them, and they will be extremely useful in the fight."

"Oh, I agree entirely," says Cromwell. "I shall set them new directives to defend this city from the invaders. They will work in accordance with the City Guard and Stalkers. But just keep in mind, Cornelia, that they operate under my design. If anything should happen to me, then they will revert to their default setting, as will the Stalkers. I would suggest it's in your best interests to keep me alive and at full health. Perhaps letting me return to Inner Haven is a good idea…"

"No," says my grandmother immediately. "You'll stay here for now. Don't worry, I'm sure your protective unit of Stalkers will keep you from harm."

"For both our sakes, I hope so too."

I listen to the exchange with a progressive drooping of the head and eyelids, my body hardly able to stay standing. Beside me, Adryan takes note and draws his arm around my waist to steady me.

"You should get some rest, Brie," he whispers. "You're not much use sleeping on your feet."

He smiles warmly as the conversation draws to a close and we begin to disband. Cromwell, Woolf, and the Consortium head for their new digs, while Zander sets about meeting with Rycard and Freya to hear further updates on the city's defences. My grandmother, meanwhile, stays at the front for a while longer, telling me, as Adryan did, that I need to sleep.

I don't argue, despite my hatred of being left out, and quickly head back to Inner Haven with Adryan by my side. I find the inner streets at the core of the city busier than ever, all those still situated in Outer Haven continuing to be brought further to the centre for their protection.

And it seems, given the threat, that some are even choosing to fight, weapons being handed out for the reserve forces, untrained men and women of both the Enhanced and Unenhanced, the last line of defence should we need them.

I hope, of course, it won't come to that. And I'm sure they do too.

I get my wish when I return to the City Guard HQ. Though a new day is dawning, and I'm sure Adryan has had about as much sleep as me, I know he can't rest. Yet he gives me some moments of comfort at least, lying beside me as I drop off, stroking my hair and warding off the demons in my mind as I drop off to sleep.

It is the peace I need. Here, on the second floor, it's all so quiet and still. And with Adryan lying beside me, coaxing me to sleep, it's a little bit of heaven in a world that's turning to hell.

CHAPTER THIRTEEN

I wake to good news.

Shaken awake by Adryan, I have no idea how long he stayed with me or how long I've been out. 'A good few hours' is all I get, and heading back outside, the shape of the sun, curving through mid afternoon, suggests I've had a long enough stretch of slumber to reinvigorate me. Still, though, I feel pretty groggy…

The news, however, is that a good proportion of our men from the battle in the woods have survived. Over the course of the last few hours, they've been coming through the gates in ones, twos and other little groups, and the final tally is that, aside from Beckett, another eight hybrids lost their lives. From a count of fifty, it appears that we fared marginally better than the Stalkers, who lost about ten.

In addition, it seems that Rhoth did indeed make it too. Along with West and Larsson, he and the vast majority of his hunters made it back. Apparently, Rhoth knows the woods far too well to be caught out, even by an outfit far stronger than his own. Escaping the battle, all the Fangs regrouped and set about taking an alternative route to the city, hence their late arrival. In the end, about ninety of the hundred made it, all of them now gathering in the southern quarter to be reunited with the rest of the tribe.

Word of the battle at the edge of the wood has quickly spread throughout the morning. I find Tess and Mrs Carmichael at their usual posts in Compton's Hall, the space now seeming to take on several more people as the central core of the city swells. They come to me seeking word on what's going on and to confirm the latest reports, and I tell them without any veil over my words.

I don't try to hide the fact that we're under serious threat here. Yet it's only to them I tell the truth, and not the kids who hassle me for information. It's best, I know, for the youngsters to stay a little in the dark, if only to make Brenda and Tess's job of looking after them easier.

As the day goes on, however, the sight of the horizon to the west, packed with a thick sheet of black smoke, is enough to set the city on edge. The woods continue to burn, the flames spreading fast and far through the night and all through the day, now growing ever closer to the western edge of the city.

Even here, in Inner Haven, the black swamp is just about visible, thickening and creeping ever closer with each passing hour. Soon, perhaps, the flames will appear too, and the fumes will begin to seep into the city itself, covering us all in a coating of soot and ash that will call a start to the now-inevitable siege.

All over the city, the people I care for have their posts. Here in Compton's Hall, my adopted mother and oldest friend, and the kids who I've lived with for many years. In the southern quarter now, the Fangs take refuge, seen to by Sophie. In the HQ, Adryan has his post, alongside my grandmother. Yet such times call for her to be seen by the people, and to go regularly to the western quarter to speak with her old husband.

And my brother, along with Rycard and Commander Burns, moving back and forward across the city, arranging the defences, liaising with our counterparts turned allies.

A lot happens that day, much of it while I slept, and plenty more when I wake. I learn too that the Con-Cops have left the eastern quarter, and have now been divided up into their companies and battalions to be assigned to operate under the orders of the City Guards and Stalkers, and our own forces of the Nameless.

In total, our numbers almost match those of the approaching army, yet many thousands of our force is made up of the Con-Cops, soldiers who operate without fear for their lives, but who are little more than cannon fodder in the face of more powerful men.

I've seen before how they fight, and even with so little training have been able to dispatch large groups of them with relative ease. They give us numbers, yes, but should we be facing an army of Enhanced and hybrids, they may have little effect other than to provide distraction and to draw fire.

Still, we have to hope that our enemy have a great deal of Unenhanced with them too. Warriors, perhaps, and those used to fighting, but not all with enhancements useful for combat. Our trump card, really, is the fact that we're here, in the city, behind tall and thick stone and metal walls, fortified and littered with gun placements and topped with guards capable of firing with a great deal of accuracy. And our weaponry, too, is far more advanced from the brief look I got at the Cure's weapons in the woods, our men fitted with pulse rifles and armour capable of deflecting and even stopping certain rounds fired from their more antique firearms.

I have to consider that what Zander said to Cromwell was true. That without their Elementals in play, without their use of fire, we'd have defeated their forward force in the woods, and this entire, looming battle would seem a lot less foreboding.

Now, the waiting game is on. With the flames growing closer, and acting as a timer for the countdown to war, the city spends its time battening down the hatches and making itself ready. All over Outer Haven now, large units of our men patrol and lie in wait, mixtures of Nameless and City Guards, Stalkers and Con-Cops. They're set to each gate, with vehicles ready to transport our soldiers to any point of the wall considered to be under threat.

Yet it's the western gate and the walls around it that draw the largest and most potent force. Within the outer districts of the western quarter, several thousand men wait, our finest snipers up on the walls, our best scouts set out in the woods, relaying information back to ensure we're not taken off guard.

My assignment has me right there next to my brother, Zander unwilling to have me anywhere but by his side. I go about the city with him, watching him work, seeing how well he leads. I'm fully aware that the soldiers of the Nameless look up to him and respect him a great deal, despite his callow years. Yet the City Guards are already doing the same, happy to take orders from the young man at such times, his authority not only ordained by the likes of Lady Orlando, and even Director Cromwell, but earned through his experience and the heroic feats he's achieved.

With Commander Burns now freeing himself from his self-imposed watch down in the infirmary, he operates from the foyer of the City Guard HQ, stepping back to the summit of the city's primary force of soldiers. Rycard did a fantastic job assimilating so many City Guards into our cause, but now Burns is back to manage the entire affair, with Rycard, along with other influential figures set to lead some of our units around the city.

Among them are both Magnus and Titus, the two towering Brutes heavily involved from the start when the transition took place, and the Nameless took control of Inner Haven. Both command their own troops, set over in the west among the more powerful units we have at our disposal. And Freya too, who's done such a good helping to bolster the city's defences, now takes up permanent position in the west, some of our better soldiers among the

Nameless under her command.

My role alongside Zander isn't a complicated one really. I am here to fight, just like everyone else, and follow orders. I don't give them, and certainly have no authority to lead. And though my recent activities have made me somewhat notorious throughout all parts and among all groups in the city, I'm not yet in a position to command anyone other than myself. And, well, even that's doubtful.

Instead, I support Zander as the days pass, and the tide of war sweeps inexorably towards us. For two days, we rush about the city from corner to corner, making sure things are in good working order, liaising with the various commanders who control the different units.

War councils are held where information is shared, and the latest intel of our scouts is brought to the leaders of the city's defence. Mostly, we all gather in the western quarter where Cromwell and his people reside. An office is set up for the purposes of plotting our course, both regarding securing the city from the invaders, and breaking apart their lines.

All appear to operate on the same wavelength now. There's little dissent or disagreement, and my grandparents appear to have put aside all of their many issues to ensure that our survival is well managed and efficiently achieved. Looking upon them, and the other commanding officers like Burns and Hatcher, as well as the thousands of hard-nosed soldiers I've seen all over the city, I begin to grow quite confident that the Cure are about to bite off more than they can chew.

Sure, they can set a wall of flame to the woods, and force us to withdraw. But here, locked outside the city with no way in? I can only imagine that they'll break against the wall likes waves on rock if they really try to breach our defences.

It seems that my grandfather has indeed been quietly preparing for the possibility of defending the city for some time. I do recall, as a young girl, how the walls were built higher back then, the gates thicker. Even now, all the gun placements being fixed and attached have been manufactured for the very specific task of warding off a threat. His foresight may just prove the very thing that saves us.

And so the days go, with the nights bringing me back to my personal haven up on level 2 of the City Guard HQ. And each night, Adryan comes to stay with me, our bodies wrapped tight and warm, with a growing feeling of safety and security starting to burgeon inside me.

I lie with him and we share so few words, our waking hours long and arduous to the point where we wish those we spend together to be silent and still. It is a silence of comfort, though, with Adryan. He's become someone with whom no words are needed to ward of any awkwardness. I can lie there and look at his face, handsome and smooth, yet creased now with the worries and minor scars inflicted by these terrible days, and merely enjoy the moment without the need to draw my voice to the room.

We share time in a period of our lives when it is in such short supply. And at any point, we know he might be summoned to my grandmother's side, or I might by summoned to my brother's. Or perhaps both of us, summoned from slumber by the drums of war, Adryan acting the intelligence officer, coordinating troop movements, me the soldier, down on the ground doing the killing.

We have such different vantages of this war, and come from such different backgrounds. And yet here, we lie together and try to press it all away to the backs of our minds. Here, in this room, during these dark days, Adryan is the light that shines.

CHAPTER FOURTEEN

Two days after the fight at the edge of the woods, the flames still rise high. They're close now, close enough to be seen from Outer Haven at high enough vantage points, the woods being swiftly eaten away with nothing but black ash left behind.

Way back from the wall, I gather with the leaders of the city's defence in the office assigned for the war council. The last couple of days have seen regular meetings take place, but until now we've had little to go on regarding enemy troop movements, except the fact that the main army has now crossed the plains and is about to begin its long trek across the scorched, blackened earth.

According to our scouts, the Cure have up until this point been moving as a single mass, aside from the advance force sent ahead to clear the woods. Now, though, it appears as though they're breaking up.

"I've had a couple of reports that smaller contingents of the enemy have been heading southeast and northeast from the main army," Colonel Hatcher informs us, the information provided by some of his more evasive and elusive Stalker scouts. "It appears that they're getting ready to assault the city from various angles."

"Not surprising at all," says Zander, growing into his role and a regular contributor in such meetings. "To attack from a single angle would have been easier to defend. They must know this."

"There is more troubling news than that," continues Hatcher. "I have lost contact with a couple of other scouts, and that can only mean one thing."

"They're dead," grunts Freya, stating the obvious.

"Worse," says Hatcher, looking around the room. "They will likely have been caught and therefore had their minds excavated. It will present the enemy with greater knowledge of our fortifications and weak points."

"Then we fortify them further," suggests Freya, expert in such things as she is.

Cromwell's voice enters the room before Hatcher can speak. It draws a hush as always.

"We have little time for that," he says. "It may be that the Cure wish for us to spread our resources more thinly. It could be a bluff."

"Bluff or not, do we have a choice?" asks Lady Orlando with her usual calm. "We can hardly allow for weak points in the wall to be found and exploited."

"We won't, Cornelia. Of course we won't. We have plenty of units capable of reaching any weak point within minutes. We have to keep our eye on the main army and not let our attention be too heavily split. If an attack comes elsewhere, we react. But I don't see how we have time to do much to the more vulnerable areas around the city."

A little more debate ensues on the matter, the issue more contentious than other points of recent discussion. Irritatingly, I actually find myself agreeing with my grandfather, his logic seeming to strike a chord with me.

In fact, this entire situation irritates me when I let myself think about it. Sure, it's great we're collaborating so well, and all over the city, the various military units on our side and theirs are working together very efficiently according to reports and what I've seen with my own eyes. But...something about that just feels off to me. It's worrying, mostly because it might well serve as a picture of the future.

Is this it from now on? If the city survives, are the remains of Cromwell's world and the burgeoning embers of our own going to merge more permanently? Already, my grandfather has all his Stalkers, Con-Cops, and loyal City Guards spread all over the city. It makes me uneasy knowing that he's planted himself here in Outer Haven so soon after being shoved out.

I brought the exact concern to my grandmother the previous day, only for her to tell me she has things in hand, and won't trust Cromwell for a second. But, actions speak louder than words, and I'm beginning to get the feeling that, under the shadow of this incoming army, the city is starting to soften to Cromwell once more, despite everything he's done.

At the end of the day, they're all just delighted to have the support of his Stalkers and other loyal soldiers. Such a situation is a dangerous one, as far as I see it. Others may let their guard down, but not me.

Not me...

The conversation moves on at a brisk pace, various opinions voiced before a conclusion is drawn and decision made. Lady Orlando may currently be the figure in the city with the most authority, but she is sensible enough to seek advice and, if needs be, defer to those with greater wisdom on matters of urban defence. It turns out, Director Cromwell is well versed in such things, given his many decades within the City Guard and, latterly, as supreme ruler of Haven.

As such, she's put in the rather unenviable position of having to listen to him, despite wishing to prevent him having too much influence. In the end, she has little choice but to trust that he knows what he's talking about, and try to ignore the niggling feeling that he has some secret agenda to further his own cause.

Thankfully, however, we have our own man with similar knowledge of managing the City Guard. While Cromwell was once Commander some time ago, that role now sits with Leyton Burns. Lady Orlando, therefore, is able to seek advice from him on the matter too, knowing he has the city's best interests at heart.

In the end, the general feeling drawn from both

men is that the city's current defensive structure is optimal. We have many units capable of moving quickly from place to place, and have ensured that the west is most heavily guarded. All possible secret routes have been booby-trapped, with the majority of the tunnels once used by the Nameless beneath the city already collapsed during our civil war. There are some left, of course, that will enable us to sneak out to sabotage the enemy, or engage in sneak attacks and ambushes if we need to, but they are both guarded and set with failsafes and explosives to ensure they cannot be used by the enemy to enter, even if they were to discover them.

Overall, the city is currently considered watertight, and the main thing to worry about is a breach in the walls or one of the gates. That, of course, is the concern – right now, we don't exactly know what capabilities the enemy has in that regard.

"They'll likely have explosive weaponry," suggests Colonel Hatcher. "The weapons they fought with in the woods were old and far less potent than what we possess. However, they didn't enter the woods with the aim of blowing it up, so we have to assume that those in the main army have weapons capable of damaging the walls."

"What sort of weapons are you talking about?" questions Lady Orlando.

"Heavy ballistics, such as grenade launchers, rocket launchers, and possibly larger, fixed position weapons with far greater capabilities. These sorts of weapons were readily available in the old world. There's no reason to think they won't have scavenged such armaments in their travels."

"And what sort of countermeasures do we have for such weapons?" Lady Orlando looks to Freya with the question.

"Our guns should have a much greater range," comes her deep, husky voice. "We can target anyone with more powerful arms…"

"And if they fire first?" cuts in Cromwell.

Freya doesn't seem to have an answer. Zander does.

"A good sniper should be able to shoot certain rocket propelled explosives from the air, exploding them before they hit the walls. Any gifted Dasher and Hawk hybrid is quite capable of that."

I think of one such hybrid, Astor, who I first met when he was acting bodyguard to Walter, the Nameless' resident chemist and drug-maker. Not so long ago I saw him shoot a whole set of drones from the sky with incredible speed and precision. I've no doubt that soldiers and snipers such as him will be able to shoot rockets from the air, even if our mobile gun placements can't.

"The problem, again," says Hatcher, "is numbers. "Other than the overall size of their army, we have so little to go on regarding the sorts of arms they're carrying, and just how many hybrids or Enhanced they have. Most of what we're discussing here is speculation. All we can really do is set the defence of this city. That is on our end, and under our control. What they can do, and the arms they have, isn't yet known to us. And we may not find out until they arrive."

His words are somewhat sobering and entirely accurate. Colonel Hatcher is a man who doesn't mince words or beat around the bush. He is, against all expectation, a man I'd happily follow to battle. It's so odd for me to think that, given his role within my grandfather's system, but Hatcher really doesn't seem so bad at all.

"Colonel Hatcher is right," says Cromwell. "We have no choice now but to wait. Preparations have been made. I commend you all for the parts you've played so far, but the true test is yet to come."

His words suggest this latest meeting is set to conclude. Always, the Director seeks to have the final word, and always Lady Orlando refuses to give it to him. It seems she has a chronic inability to give him any measure of his old authority here, an authority that she now possesses.

"And negotiation?" she asks suddenly, just as people prepare to move off. "I've been giving the option some further thought. What harm is there in sending an envoy to find out just what they want?"

"Harm?" huffs Cromwell, eyes tilting into a frown I take for mocking. "The harm, dear Cornelia, will be done to whatever poor soul you choose to send. They will be killed, of course. But worse for us all, their minds will be examined for information first. There is nothing to be achieved from doing such a thing."

Lady Orlando's eyes are already moving

elsewhere as he speaks, seeking out someone whose opinion she has more faith in. They start on Commander Burns, whose sharp mind is back to full fitness and ready to give the matter all due consideration.

"It does seem to me, by looking at the evidence, that we are facing an army with no desire other than our destruction." Cromwell seems pleased with the endorsement, before Burns continues. "However, diplomacy can't be discounted either. It is *logical*, after all, to consider all ends."

"Not so in this case, Leyton," counters Cromwell. "Didn't young Zander discover this army's true purpose within the mind of this messenger sent to the Fangs? Did he not confirm what I already knew – that they are barbarians who have no desire to build, but only seek to destroy? These people are at odds with our way of life here."

"Don't speak of our way of life, Artemis, as if we're all on the same page," bites Lady Orlando. "You wish only to see the Savants flourish. You care nothing for anyone else. Your world is as much about destruction as the Cure…"

"A simple and rather insipid way of putting it, Cornelia. And in any case, my plans have been forced to change. I assure you, negotiating with these people is a waste of time. There is no point in sending anyone to their death."

Once more, my grandmother shows total contempt for her old husband by turning her eyes to Zander as he speaks. Entranced by the discussion though I am,

I still manage a smirk at the look of displeasure in Cromwell's eye.

"Zander, tell us again what you saw in this man's mind?" she says.

My brother's eyes dart swiftly between the arguing parties before he begins.

"I do believe that Director Cromwell is correct," he says, semi-reluctantly. "It was a brief glimpse only, but the intent was very clear. They are coming to destroy the city entirely. I can't really imagine what speaking to them will achieve. I'm...sorry Lady Orlando."

She's already shaking her head.

"No, child, no apologies. Your opinion matters to me above all. I trust you completely. If that's truly what you saw, then I will concede. Yet it does pain me not to at least try."

A few long seconds of silence fall, an opportunity for Zander to retreat a little and agree that attempting to negotiate is still possible. He doesn't. He sticks to his convictions and beliefs, as he always seems to, even if it means siding with Cromwell ahead of her.

Eventually, the silence ends with Cromwell's crackling old voice.

"There you have it, Cornelia. The boy speaks a great deal of sense. Now let us forget this negotiation nonsense and set our minds to one end alone – eradicating these invaders."

He smiles, and this time, for the first time, has the

last word, marching straight for the door with his sycophants by his side.

CHAPTER FIFTEEN

I spend that evening with those I care about, hidden behind the walls of Inner Haven and right at the heart of the city. It is the safest place to be, far from the outer walls and incoming fight. Tess, Brenda, Abby, and even Adryan, stationed in the City Guard HQ, should be perfectly safe here.

Right now, we have entered a period that could rightly be called the calm before the storm. It is a storm we know is coming, and though the city is quiet, inside the hearts and minds of all those within it, the storm has already arrived.

I can see that from the looks in their eyes and on their faces. While the likes of Brenda and Tess have grown skilled in hiding their fears for the sake of the kids, I can see through the lies their expressions tell, and know full well that they're worried by what we face.

Sitting in the dim quiet of Compton's Hall that night, I hear about the rumours that have continued to circulate. They know, of course, that the army is coming. And they know that the woods are burning. They know, too, that we're facing a horde of ten thousand, the potency of their soldiers and warriors still unconfirmed and yet likely, by what we've seen, to present us with a major challenge.

I still hold personal faith in our defence, given what I've seen around the perimeter of Outer Haven, and the collaboration and teamwork shown by the various military strands operating in the city. But, regardless, here at the core it's almost worse. They merely sit here, day by day, and wait, with no chance to influence events as I can, in small part at least.

And those rumours, the worst ones, tell of foes that few people have ever faced. They speak of these Elementals with the power to summon the wind or spread fire through the streets. They tell of great and terrible warriors, marching through distant lands, destroying everything they see, their eyes now set on us and us alone.

The rumours are mostly embellished, typical of such things. And with fear now spreading like wildfire, creeping through quiet conversations and internal thoughts, they're only set to grow more ambitious and inaccurate.

"I heard the woods were burned down by a fire-manipulator," asks Tess, eyes carved in worry now that the kids are sleeping. "That everyone had to flee, even the Stalkers. Can a man really do that? Can he burn down an entire forest on his own?"

"He had help, Tess. There was a wind-manipulator there too, fanning the flames…"

"That's even worse!" she says. "How many of these people do you think they have?"

"Um…we have no idea I'm afraid."

"It can't be many," asserts Mrs Carmichael with the sort of confidence that suggests she's an expert on such matters. "We don't have any people like that around here. They must be very rare."

"Well, how many do you need," says Tess. "If it only takes one to burn down a forest, it only takes one to burn down a city…"

"Stone and metal doesn't burn like wood, Tess," says my guardian shaking her head. "Anyway, I'm sure Brie and her friends have plans to take down any such people before they do any real damage?"

They both look to me expectantly. I nod and smile. We have certainly assigned such people as priority targets if and when we see them. The problem is, you'd never know who they were until they set loose their powers. Our plans for them are, therefore, somewhat basic.

I also fail to mention that the woods didn't just burn, they melted. The fire wasn't ordinary fire, but an inferno hot enough to wrap up the ruins of that old town and any poor soul caught within it, quickly melting both stone, metal, and flesh alike.

That detail, I keep to myself.

During our whispered conversation, Adryan appears from the main doorway. He comes here if he gets a chance, often when I'm not even around, just to check up on my friends for me. Tonight, though, he's clearly been looking for me – usually, I'd be back in my room by now. Though, it's become *our* room recently.

"Hi everyone," he says softly, his voice carrying over to us in that vast hall. "You're up late tonight."

He takes a seat within our little circle, right up close to me. I find myself immediately shuffling a little sideways towards him and resting my head on his shoulder. His arm wraps. I could sleep right here.

"Hard to sleep now," says Tess. "You never know how many hours you've got left. Don't want to waste them."

"We'll be fine here," says Adryan. "We're perfectly safe."

He always gives the party line. I imagine that, working alongside my grandmother, he's learned that it's best to stay as upbeat as possible about our chances when speaking to civilians. He is an optimist too, I guess. So he probably does believe it.

We speak for a little while, Adryan changing the atmosphere just a little. I see Brenda looking at us sitting together with a smile, Tess taking charge of the conversation as she rattles off a bevvy of other rumours about what we're facing and the feats of those coming to kill us. Adryan fends them off skilfully, while I just stay quiet, my eyes starting to droop as my mind wanders off.

This, right here, is what I want. My guardian who raised me. My best friend. My…husband. All it would take is to add a few others – Zander, my grandmother, Drum, and my little gang would be complete. A troop of close friends and family whom I love and would do anything for. I imagine us all having dinner together, eating and laughing, a joyous affair away from war and death.

One day, maybe it will happen. But right now my imagination will have to do. Others could be invited. Rhoth and West, Sophie and Rycard, Commander Burns, Freya, Walter, Magnus and Titus. So many people from so many backgrounds have touched my life, touched this war in one way or another.

Now all wait in this city, their lives under threat. And hour by hour that threat grows near, marching across the once lush woodland turned barren and scorched, now dead and lifeless. They have killed it as they have so many other tribes and peoples across the distant lands, blackening the road ahead and coming here to do the same.

I wonder just how much of the world to the west has been similarly branded. How many people, like West's family and village, have found themselves murdered and wiped out, or assimilated into their cause. Many will no doubt fight for them against their wishes. Many of their warriors and soldiers will no doubt have been innocent people once before, living their lives, living in peace.

But, just as in this city, out there are those who can manipulate minds and turn people against their own will. People who can actively recondition others, just like my grandfather does, force people into slavery, make them do their bidding.

This army of the Cure, I'm sure, will be filled to

the brim with people forced to march so far from home. People who may have seen their friends and families die, their homes burnt to the ground. People who now live their lives in this storm of destruction, unable to break free of the constraints within their minds, forcing them to murder and kill.

I do wonder, sometimes, how many people are really evil out there. Even my grandfather, with all he's done, isn't evil for the sake of it. Adryan once said that he and the Consortium weren't evil, but were merely products of their biology and upbringing, products of the world they come from.

I wonder, then, what truly drives those who come to kill us? How many of this force of ten thousand are evil men and women? Are they merely products of a different world, forced to act by the doctrines of their own dictator? Is there a leader out there, or a group of them, who truly see Haven as a blight on this world that needs to be destroyed?

Out there, some warlords are hunting us down. And here in this city we're giving refuge to another. And should you be so inclined, you could even look at my grandmother as the same, ordering for the High Tower to be destroyed, for thousands of innocent people within it to be killed.

I have learned over these weeks and months that there is so little black and white out there. That the shades of grey dominate. In the end, all we have are our motivations, the things that drive us individually and as a collective. Right now, for the entire city, that is survival. And for me personally, it's seeing those I care about get out of this whole mess as unscathed as possible.

Some I fear for more than others, and certainly far more than I do myself. My own life and mortality has taken a back seat. I will happily use it to defend those I love, even sacrifice it if I have to.

Drum is high on that list. I have barely seen him since he returned from the mines, now assigned to some unit off in the southern quarter. I'm happy at least that he's not in the west, considered to be the most likely point of major conflict, and hope that he'll be able to watch this war pass by without being required to fight.

I've seen him once or twice on my rounds with Zander, our travels across the city bringing us into brief contact on occasion. Our greetings aren't as they used to be, though – no affection beyond stolen smiles. Within his troop he can't show weakness. We don't hug or take time alone to speak.

I have seen Rhoth and West, and the rest of the Fangs several times as well. And with them, Sophie, doing a fine job in managing such a disorderly rabble, so out of their comfort zone here in the 'big city with all the lights', a place that has held merely fear and awe for them for so many years.

Rhoth and his hunters, however, will never shy from a fight. Even after their losses against the Bear-Skins, and the ten or so men they lost in the battle at the edge of the wood, they will brush themselves off and go again. They will defend this city as if it was their own, because with their families within its walls, and their village now burned to a cinder, it's as close to a home as they'll find.

They have not been spread among the other units and troops that patrol and defend the walls, however. Rhoth's remit has been to stay within the inner districts of the southern quarter and offer protection to his people.

"If the fighting comes to you, so be it," Zander told him only yesterday. "You'll want to be here to defend your people if that happens."

"We can help defend the front," Rhoth asserted.

Zander's growing authority denied him.

"No, Rhoth. You have done more than enough already. Defend your people. We will defend the walls."

Rhoth didn't argue much more after that. And he didn't call my brother 'boy' either. The mutual respect between the two has now cast such things aside. For now, at least.

And so the land lies, all of us dispersed among the city at different points and with different orders to see through. I will follow my brother anywhere, and will no doubt see some action myself. We will fight together, hybrid twins, grandchildren of the leaders of both the Consortium and the Nameless.

And maybe tomorrow, maybe the next day, the fighting will begin.

But these stolen moments of calm are what fuel me. With the storm brewing in the west, I sit up late that night with Brenda, Tess, and Adryan, sometimes engaging in the conversation, sometimes merely dozing on Adryan's shoulder and letting my mind wander as it's prone to do.

In the dim light of the hall, with the ambient sounds of several hundred people sleeping, or whispering in groups just like ours, I let the minutes turn to hours and the hours fade away. I hold onto those moments as the clock ticks on, each second bringing the winds of war closer.

And when the morning comes, the flames that engulf the forest to the west begin to die away. They have eaten their fill, leaving behind the black earth that is nothing but a road for the incoming horde.

And those dying flames, and the black fumes that fill the sky, are a signal to anyone who can see them, from the far reaches of all corners of Outer Haven, to all those cowering at the core where the High Tower once stood.

It's a signal that the enemy have come.

It's a signal that the siege is set to begin.

CHAPTER SIXTEEN

The morning is late and the afternoon approaching when I stand at the edge of Outer Haven, on top of the wall, looking out through the battlements at the blackened shape of the earth.

What was once an endless wood, stretching for many miles to the west, south and north, is now a charred forest of burnt stumps and ash, peppered with points where the flames continue to flicker in the breeze and the embers glow red and wild.

The cloud of smoke that reaches to the air is all consuming and vast. It has now spread not only across the lands outside of the city, but to much of the city itself. The western quarter of Outer Haven, in particular, is doused in black and grey smog, the smoke only likely to drift further east as the winds distribute it far and wide.

Yet to the west it's much darker, hard for our eyes to penetrate. It is a cloak, purposely designed to help hide the force that comes our way. Even our scouts, so skilful at remaining hidden and watching from afar, have been neutered by this clear device of war. And our drones too, hovering in the sky, their cameras blinded by the smog as they watch over the city.

Here, we have no one capable of shaping the winds to blow the smoke away. And even if we did, it would take a force of them to clear out the entire city and the lands beyond. Yet through the haze, as the natural winds sweep across and help to create gaps in the shroud, the framing of bodies becomes clear to my Hawk eyes.

Searching forward, I think I see them, still some distance away. A mass of shapes, of men and women, rippling like waves of heat on a sweltering day as they press forward. But the glimpses are rare, images quickly snatched away as more black smoke blows in and hides them once more.

Down beyond the wall at the gate, the cloud is being discussed. I quickly move from the top of the battlements and join the commanders. Zander turns to me.

"What did you see?" he asks.

"They're coming," I tell him, confirming what we already know and what other Hawks have said. "Miles out still, but I saw them."

"The whole army?" asks Colonel Hatcher.

"Just a sea of bodies and shapes," I say, shaking my head. "It's impossible to tell."

"This cloud," says Ryard, right there along with us and setting his one good eye to the black sky. "It needs to go."

"And what can we do?" questions Hatcher. "There's nothing to be done about it but let it clear of its own accord."

Unfortunately, that might not be so easy. The fumes remain thick enough to last for some time yet unless a ferocious set of strong winds should come and dismiss it. And even then, the wind-manipulators among the enemy horde might just seek to hold the cloud where it is, keep the city locked in perpetual darkness to hide their movements.

We're all quite aware that that's just what they're doing. Burning the woods seemed to always be the plan, serving the two-fold purpose of clearing their path and hiding their step. Now, our defences are somewhat muted. If we can't see them, how exactly can we fight them?

"How about your scouts to the south and north?" asks Commander Burns, looking at Colonel Hatcher. "Have they spotted further enemy movements in the regions?"

Hatcher shakes his head.

"Nothing new to report, but we've been forced to withdraw some of them due to poor visibility. They can't operate at their optimum levels in this smog, Commander."

"And our drones?"

"The same. Any of them we send out get shot straight down. The smoke is too thick for them to operate in effectively now."

"Then they have us sitting here blind," says Burns. "We need to know where they'll strike. Set further watches to the battlements in the north and south.

We need as many eyes up high as we can get…"

"Sir, there are no more eyes to give," says Zander. "All Hawks are set in position and watching the lands outside the walls. All avenues are covered. But this smoke makes anything else impossible. We can't do much more."

"All we can do is wait," says Hatcher. "And pray for a storm."

The anxiety among the commanders is obvious. Even those so calm and cool in all scenarios are now growing strained by this new development. And even as we speak, more fumes seem to pour in, and the visibility within the city seems to grow worse. In a few hours time, all of Haven might be buried by it, the flames now working their way towards the northern woods at the base of the mountains where the Bear-Skins dwell.

"OK, I'll report to Lady Orlando," says Burns. "Do the same with Director Cromwell."

Colonel Hatcher nods and marches off to the control room outside the western gate. Commander Burns heads straight for his vehicle, to be quickly chauffeured through the empty streets towards Inner Haven. Only Rycard, Zander, Freya and me are left, the half-Hawk and half-Brute quick to set about relaying orders to their troops.

I feel somewhat impotent at times like this. I have no unit to command, and am little more than a sidekick to my brother, keeping to his flank as we sweep around, maintaining morale and informing the various commanders of the latest developments.

Zander's role seems to be as liaison and motivator-in-chief, working just beneath Commander Burns and Colonel Hatcher, and without a unit of his own to command. His role is more free-roaming, set to go where the action is thickest. And I'll be right there beside him at all times.

He's long given up trying to keep me safe from harm. He knows that's not possible now. Instead, I guess we'll be best suited working together. And I want to keep an eye on him as much as he does me.

The tension among the soldiers around the western gate grows more pronounced as the afternoon marches on. At any moment, we know that a strike could come from ahead, or any other point around the city's perimeter. Everyone is on edge. Everyone primed to fight.

And it's the waiting that's the worst thing of all.

But while we cannot see much through the smog, there's little the Cure can do to shield themselves from the ears of the Bats that spread around the walls. The eyes of the Hawks can be blinded. The noses of the Sniffers can be confounded by the fumes. But the march of so many men, and their stamping feet cracking through the burnt brush, is clear as day to those with augmented hearing.

They are the first to know that a force of thousands is on its way, and can even pinpoint just how far they are from the walls. But before too long, even those of us with unaugmented ears are able to note the rumble from afar, and even the deaf would be able to perceive the trembling of the earth as they grow near.

They're less than a mile away, the Bats tell us, suggesting that the vast majority of the army remains as one. It seems they haven't yet splintered, apart from the smaller contingents spotted moving south and north.

As they continue on, and the distant drum of several thousand feet grows louder, orders are given to set the giant guns on the battlements on them. Their range is a thousand metres, some shooting large explosive shells, others rounds of energy just like our pulse rifles. As soon as the enemy get with a kilometre, they'll be stepping into a world of pain.

But they don't.

As the Bats listen closely, calling down their estimations of how far the Cure are from the walls, one suddenly shouts out that they've stopped.

"How far?" demands Commander Burns, having quickly returned from Inner Haven.

"Just beyond the thousand metre mark," says the soldier. "They've stopped just out of range, sir."

Burns lifts a wry smile that only a man of such composure could at a time like this.

"They know our capabilities," he says. "They know just how far we can shoot."

"We should fire anyway," suggest Freya. "The Bats might be wrong."

"They're not wrong," asserts Colonel Hatcher. I can tell he's got Bat powers himself. He tilts his head slightly, and listens closely. "No, there's no point in firing, not yet."

"Then what now?" asks Freya, her white eyebrows pressed into a ferocious frown.

"We do the same as we've been doing all day," says Burns. "We wait, and see what they do. The ball is in their court."

It is, and it's worrying that they're so skilled at the game. What we thought to be a murderous horde of barbarians has proven itself something far more. They're organised. They have some extremely powerful hybrids and enhanced among them. And now we're fully aware that they know just what our defences are capable of.

So we wait, and the Bats continue to listen for movement. Nothing happens, not for hours as the fumes grow stronger, and the light fades, the dark of night and the shroud of smoke conspiring to turn the world as black as tar.

"They're waiting for optimum conditions," Zander suggests. "When we can't see a thing…that's when they'll strike."

His words are ominous, and thoughts shared by all. We wait, ready, expecting the worst, expecting anything. Then from the top of the wall, a soldier calls.

"Movement! I have movement!"

I feel my muscles tense, my vision sharpen. Any second now, the big guns will surely go off, sending deadly shells and blasts of burning energy out into the darkening night.

But no, the guns don't fire. The movement isn't of the masses, still camped and waiting over a kilometre away. It belongs only to several men, the crunching footsteps creeping to the keenest of ears only.

Our chief listener, our most powerful Bat, is the one who spots them. His words draw us up to the battlements. I follow my brother up the stairs constructed behind the wall, right to the summit where our soldiers wait behind shields of metal, eyes searching through strips.

We approach the Bat as quickly and quietly as possible. Hatcher comes with us, and Rycard too. Burns and Freya remain on the ground. My grandparents are both absent, leaving their commanders to run the city's defence right here as they operate further behind the lines.

"Who is it?" questions Zander. "Who's coming?"

The Bat listens once more, and I notice Colonel Hatcher doing the same. Both shut their eyes and then Hatcher speaks.

"Four of them," he says. "Four people only, walking right to the gate. No more than fifty metres out."

The main Bat confirms, nodding. We wait, the Hawks now searching as far as possible through the smoky night. Less than a minute later, the four shadows are appearing, emerging from the shroud, walking calmly, casually, right for the gate just as

Hatcher said.

Then I hear him whisper, just as I take in the outlines of the men.

"Our scouts," he says. "They're our missing scouts…"

A ripple of tension spreads down the line of soldiers manning the wall. Dressed in the black cloaks of the Stalkers, the scouts walk in a line, close together, expressions placid and eyes dark.

Hatcher calls from the wall.

"Stop right there," he says to his men.

The Stalker scouts do as commanded.

"Should we open the gate," I ask. "Let them back in?"

Colonel Hatcher shakes his head.

"No. We can't. This is a trap and nothing more. These men are already dead."

His words are loud enough to be heard by the scouts. The manner in which they react sets my teeth on edge.

Even through the darkness, the shapes of their mouths, curling into smiles, are clear. They all do so as one, and all lift their chins and speak together.

"The city of Haven is doomed," they drone. "All who wish to live, flee this night. This is your final chance. Leave, and we will not pursue you. Stay, and all will die within your walls…"

Their words fade and melt into the silence. No one

moves or stirs. No one says a word.

Then Colonel Hatcher turns his eyes left, then right, drawing the gaze of the soldiers on the battlements.

"They're under the spell of the enemy now," he says steadily, his voice slicing through the silence. "On my command, kill them."

The Stalkers must hear, but none of them move. They just stand there, rigid, as our men lift their rifles and aim, locked in place by whatever order has been set to their minds. Hatcher raises his hand, holds it for a second, then drops it straight down to his side.

And as he does, several dozen guns go off, peppering the four Stalkers with rounds of red and blue and green. The black of their outfits lights up, and I see their faces before they fall. None are afraid. None are in pain. They have delivered their message and served their purpose. The enemy needs them no more.

They hit the earth and sink into heaps of burning flesh, four more of those tasked with defending the city now lost. And in my head, their words echo, and my faith that this city will survive continues to erode.

Zander must know that we're all thinking the same. He must see it in the people's eyes. Because it's his voice that sounds now, bellowing out loudly, spreading down the lines.

"These barbarians are trying to frighten us," he

shouts. "They're trying to make us cower behind these walls and doubt in our defences. We will do nothing of the sort! When they come, we will destroy them. They will not make good their threats!"

His words bring some murmuring of assent, and I see eyes imbued with a fresh dose of hope. It's what Zander does well, inspiring the soldiers, many of whom have long worked under his guidance and command.

He may just be a boy, not yet nineteen years of age, but he's lived through enough battle and war for several seasoned men. He will stand here at the gates, and dare anyone to pass if they wish to kill those who cower behind. And right alongside him, the soldiers will be.

Right alongside him, I'll be.

CHAPTER SEVENTEEN

That night, as the bodies of the Stalker scouts burn outside our doors, no word is passed to Inner Haven about they message they were sent to bring.

"If anyone leaves the city, they'll be killed or be added to the Cure's ranks," Commander Burns tells us. We're all in agreement on that point. "I suspect this is a plot they've used before. The people are safer at the core of this city than out there beyond the walls."

"I agree entirely, Commander Burns," says Colonel Hatcher. "If we die here, then we *all* die here. There's no escaping this threat out in the burning wilds."

"It could also be a ploy to distract us," says Zander. "They said 'flee this night', which suggests they won't attack until tomorrow at the earliest..."

"We can't read anything into that," says Hatcher. "They could attack at any moment."

"Yeah, that's what I'm getting at, Colonel."

"Well good, let them come and get it over with," grunts Freya. "All this waiting around bores me."

"I'm sure you'll get plenty of excitement soon enough," says Burns.

"Good. Bring it on."

I smile at the gigantic woman. It's just the sort of attitude we like to see around here.

I'm of much the same disposition. There's little worse than the waiting and the wondering. It gives you time to think, time to worry, time to fear, if not for yourself, then for those you care for. Our preparations have been made, and time won't serve us anymore. In fact, it will only serve the enemy.

Because as time passes that night, the skies darken to a shade hitherto unforeseen in this city. Not since the dark days of so long ago has the world been so blackened. The thick fume spreads and chokes us, and all light from the skies above, from the moon and stars, is blotted and quenched. Whether there are clouds up there, I don't even know. The fog of smoke, of war, is enough to cast the city in a deep and impenetrable shroud.

Before too long, it's hard to see more than a dozen or so metres ahead. From the top of the wall, our Hawks are made redundant. Try as they might to see through the smog, their eyes rely on clear air. Normal darkness doesn't affect them, but this darkness is far from normal.

It is by design, unnatural. Our enemy can control the elements, turn day to night. They can take away our powers, alter the conditions to suit their needs. Our Hawks cannot see. Our Sniffers cannot smell. And soon enough, they'll show us that they can eliminate our Bats from the picture too.

It happens several hours past midnight, at a time

when many of us begin to think that our enemy are resting. That they're likely to wait for the next day, or the next night, to strike. It's a hope, rather than an expectation. And so it soon proves.

With our Bats all listening closely for movement, and no word coming from them that the enemy is on the march, a piercing, screeching sound fills the air.

It's high pitched and unpleasant to my ears, as it is to all those with regular hearing. Yet it isn't intended for us, but for the Bats. I see their faces coil in discomfort, their shoulders hunch and eyes close tight. The noise seems to come from various points, right ahead of us to the west, but to the north and south too, closing us into a vise of sonic blasts.

It takes several moments for us to realise just what they're doing. To realise that the smaller forces sent off to the north and south, those who broke away from the main army, had a specific task in mind. That the Cure have designed or discovered in the ruins of the old world machines that can negate the specialised hearing of our Bats, as much as the smoke negates the Hawks' sight and the Sniffers' smell.

The sound is constant and unending, enough to distract our Bats from all other movement. We can no longer see or smell or hear them coming. Our Enhanced have been neutralised.

The movement behind the gate is now frantic. As we begin to realise what's going on, our commanders quickly send word to all units around the city to prepare for an imminent attack.

It might now come from any angle. Hidden by the smoke and shrieking sound, we cannot tell where the enemy is. Are they moving for the gate right now, as one? Are they splitting, hurrying off under cover to various weak points around our walls?

We quickly huddle into a group and consider the options. A round of debate rushes, louder and faster than usual, all of us wincing at the noise and none more so than Colonel Hatcher.

"We should fire immediately!" shouts Rycard. "Light the bastards up!"

"We don't even know if they're moving yet," counters Commander Burns. "We can ill afford to waste ammunition."

"With all due respect, sir, we can ill afford to let them wander towards the walls unchallenged," says Rycard. "Fire at them, show them there's no way through. Show them what we're made of."

"Who agrees?" asks Burns, looking around the group.

Freya nods. Zander nods. I do too.

Colonel Hatcher has the final word.

"Unfortunately," he begins, grimacing, "I think the enemy know what we're made of already. They clearly know our range. They know how to neutralise our defences so we can't see them coming. We can fire, but we'll be doing so blindly without knowing what success we're having. I say fire warning shots but nothing more. As Commander Burns says, we cannot waste ammunition."

"Good," says Burns. "Give the order, Colonel. And get some drones out there too…"

"Sir, they cannot operate in this smoke," says Rycard.

"I know. Keep them low to the ground. I don't care if they're destroyed. They'll give us some warning at least that the enemy is coming. Order all units along the perimeter to send them out."

"Yes, sir," nods Rycard, rushing off.

The order for warning shots is given, and I wait nervously as the large guns shift positions and prepare to fire. Above the incessant wailing, loud booms suddenly strike out, and fizzing balls of energy spread off into the mist. I watch them go from up on the battlements, and see them reach their targets hundreds of metres away, helping light up the world just a little as they go hunting.

And when they explode, about a kilometre out, I feel my heart suddenly lurch. They light up the world around them, and I see the army of the Cure still waiting out of reach. But now, the mass has shrunk. The army has split.

They're breaking up and on the move.

"Impact, a thousand metres out," calls a soldier. "No hit."

I rush back down.

"They're splitting apart. They're not stupid enough to walk straight into the path of our guns!

We have to bolster positions to the north and south."

"I agree, Commander Burns," says Zander. "They're clearly not going to strike here."

"Or it could be a double bluff," says Burns. "Lure our forces elsewhere and then bring the attack here to the western gate."

"Maybe, but we can't wait to find out."

"I happen to agree," says Burns after a moment of consideration. "Head to the south, Zander. I'll send Hatcher north. Our mobile units are on hand to move as soon as they need to."

Zander nods and, without delay, begins rushing off towards a jeep as I trail in his wake. We jump inside, the drive to the southern gate at least five minutes long even through clear streets and with Zander's foot refusing to ease up on the gas.

We pass numerous security points as we go, the outer districts around the entire perimeter of Outer Haven all fitted with patrols of men, some large and some small. They're more fortified closer to the wall, some containing groupings of several hundred soldiers, all ready to rush to the action if called up.

They see us coming through the shroud, and know we're not to be disturbed as we rush through, sirens blaring. Already, all patrols, units, and security cordons have been informed of what's happening, communication between the city's military extremely efficient.

It's so dark and so misty that I can barely imagine driving this fast myself, the ends of roads and other obstacles quickly appearing before my brother's eyes. He's quick enough to react, his knowledge of the upper streets of the city just as good as that of the underlands. It allows us to travel at a tremendous pace, working through the fastest route heading southeast from the western gate.

Arriving, we find several units in place, though the fortifications here aren't quite as dramatic. There are fixed units of soldiers, mostly City Guards with our own soldiers of the Nameless, as well as Con-Cops for backup and support. Peppered around are the Stalkers and our hybrids, most of them stationed at the front line unless they're assigned to the protection of Cromwell or, in the case of Marler, Lady Orlando. Despite Marler's soldiery skills, he's been kept back for now, right at my grandmother's side in Inner Haven.

Drum, I know, is stationed further back from the wall not too far from here. What I considered a rather safe posting has now become a little more fraught with danger. Should the city come under siege right here, the likes of Drum may be called up to join the fight.

Still, I really have no time whatsoever to spare for worrying right now. The world is simply too hectic, too loud, too dark, and too confusing to give me any space or time to think beyond the current actions I'm taking. I've never given much credence to the old, ancient phrase 'to live for the moment', but right now I'm certainly living within it.

I'm going from one moment to the next without thinking beyond that narrow scope.

All over the city now, we're bracing for an imminent attack. It could come at any time and from anywhere. We might be right in the thick of the action here, with a thousand men just outside the gate. Or we could be as far from it as possible, the northern gate about to be besieged.

All we have are the drones sent out now to give some warning. Operating in silent mode, they slip from the tops of the walls, drift down low to the ground, and begin hovering through the smoky air, spreading out from the perimeter in a bid to find our enemy.

Marching into the control room beside the southern gate, we find a set of monitors set up, soldiers watching the feed from the security cameras on the drones, once used to keep a watch over the Unenhanced in Outer Haven, and now retrofitted for war.

Dozens of them move off, their lights doused and shut off, yet their little motors unable to be quietened. Most Bats would hear them coming a mile off, but perhaps with this endless wailing from beyond our borders, our enemy won't hear them approach.

The monitors show little more than black. Thick smoke hovers above the ground, obscuring all sight any further than a half dozen metres from the drones. Another monitor has each of them positioned on a map, little red dots to denote their positions as they buzz away into the murky night, seeking out their prey.

They move twenty metres from the wall, forty, sixty, and find nothing but the burnt embers of the forest, still breathing heavy fumes to the sky. The tension, as we watch, is almost unbearable. Soon, the drones are spreading over a hundred metres from the perimeter and have found and seen nothing.

They go another hundred metres, and still nothing. The soldiers begin to wonder whether the attack is set to happen here.

Then, suddenly, a radio bursts to life, and voices clatter down the line. It has us jumping as we lose focus on the monitors, and hear our allies over in the north calling out that an attack is imminent.

"Soldiers spotted," crackles the voice over the endless din. "Hundreds of them…approaching fast…guns ready to fire…"

Across the city, several loud booms rumble, and a split second later we hear them on the radio, sending blasts of static our way. Then gunfire, crackling, spitting, several miles from here. But not just at the northern gate. We hear it further west as well, and then not far from where we stand.

Our eyes are drawn back to the monitor by a soldier.

"Sir! Zander!" he calls out.

We look again, and see that several of the drones are going dark. One after another, the camera feeds are cut off, monitor after monitor cutting to black. And as they do, the little red lights on the map disappear. One by one, they go out.

Two hundred metres from the wall, all the way along the perimeter of the south, the drones are taken out. Without delay, Zander orders for the guns to fire at the drones' last positions.

"Fire now," he shouts, pointing at the map as the red lights fade. "Fire!

He rushes outside, and I follow. We dash to the top of the wall just as the booming guns go off, joining the various others now defending the city from a multi-pronged assault. I see the shells spread and the balls of energy fizz, lighting up the world, hitting the earth two hundred metres out.

And this time, I don't just see a mass of shapes beyond, just out of reach.

I see them rushing forward, firing as they go. Hundreds of them, peppering us, not just with regular rounds, but fizzing explosives too. Zander grabs me and drags me down, and the shields and battlements at the summit of the wall start to rattle and pop as a thousand bullets come calling.

And lower down, rumbles shake the foundations as explosives hit the stone and brick, biting off chunks, eating their way through the structure that keeps the city safe.

The wall that has, for so long, stood tall and kept the outside world at bay. But now, that outside world has gathered. That outside world has brought the fight to us.

CHAPTER EIGHTEEN

Atop the wall, we fire blindly, hidden away in safety behind the thick protective shields. A hundred pulse rifles, manning the southern gate and the walls either side, split out into the night and give frame to the world. And the larger guns shout out loud, turning the lands just beyond our borders into a cauldron of fire and death.

But the enemy remain unseen, hidden amidst the smog. They appear in flashes when our guns hunt them down, but disappear just as fast. Then more flashes light up the night, and I see bodies in the dirt. Not many, but some. Perhaps attacking here was foolish after all.

The attack doesn't last long, however. The sudden barrage of bullets from the Cure, and the fizzing explosive missiles that crunch into the walls, do little more than superficial damage. Our Hawks and snipers, thought to be able to shoot the bombs down, see them too late as they emerge from the shroud. Some fire them from the sky, but most hit their mark. But, unexpectedly, their effect seems to be minimal.

It appears the walls are too sturdily built, too strong for such weaponry, scavenged from the old world and unable to compete with the new. The enemy seem to realise it, their sudden attack fading almost as fast as it began.

All over the city, the same appears to happen. Not just here, but in the west and north too, a lull seems to drop. And the east, as yet unattacked if my ears don't deceive me, the enemy yet to venture that far.

A quiet falls, and I feel the blood pump harder in my ears. Then Zander whispers.

"They're testing the defences," he says. "We need to be ready to displace…"

He moves straight off, down behind the gate, and I follow. Into the control room we go, and he says the same to the men on the radios.

"We're too strong here," he says. "They're going to attack elsewhere. Inform Commander Burns and Colonel Hatcher."

The technician nods.

"Sir, they've already called in. They said the same."

"Good. Then we're on the same wavelength."

We head back outside, the space behind the gate filled with a vast collection of vehicles, both military and civilian, ready to take our soldiers wherever they need to go.

The call comes quickly. To the south of the gate, a sudden burst of noise lifts once more. I see, in the distance, a shroud of yellow and orange begin to burn in the mist, and know that the wall is being besieged. A couple of booming shots fire from guns fixed in the area, though our defences there are weaker. We jump into a vehicle, and speed along the road along with several other mobile units. By the time we arrive, however, the fighting has once more ceased.

For the next hour, the same thing occurs again and again. Every few minutes, a new bout of fighting fills the air from various corners of the city, the perimeter being continually tested, stretching our defences. We lose men atop the walls, but only a few, and for the most part the ramparts hold firm, weakened in places but not enough to cause a breach.

And all the while, that wailing noise continues to batter our ears, a constant burden, and the smoke continues to seep up our noses and tickle our eyes, forcing many to pull on their gas masks in response.

We rush about, moving east and west along the southern perimeter of the city, rarely arriving in time to make a difference. It is a game of cat and mouse, and the Cure are the former. Toying with us, testing us, they never attack for long. Sniping in and out, they nibble and bite at our extremities, drawing blood from minor wounds but never going for the killing stroke.

I would take it for a botched siege, but I know it's nothing of the sort. This is a plan of theirs, a very specific strategy. They have neutralised our Enhanced, our ability to see and hear and smell them coming. Now they know just where our defences are strongest, and have begun the process of weakening the walls, and tiring our soldiers.

With the constant wailing, and the debilitating smoke, our men will start to suffer. The Cure know this. They have designed this. This is not a botched siege at all, but a strategy to weaken us, exhaust us, pull us left and right and wait for the perfect time to strike.

I doubt they've ever attacked a city like this before. Though my eyes have been opened to what else exists out there, I'm certain there's no place quite like Haven. Yet they clearly know how to destroy and pillage. It is their life's work, their profession. And this is their career defining moment.

The night is long, longer perhaps than any I've ever endured. It drains us all, both physically and emotionally, the constant exertions of wondering when the next attack will come, rushing about should a breach occur, serving to bleed us dry of what energy we have.

We lose men, shot from the ramparts or caught in explosions, but must surely take more. Each time I find myself moving to the summit and looking out beyond the city, I see bodies in the dirt, and begin to think that they must be little more than cannon fodder, expendables, send ahead to test us, perhaps draw us into a false sense of security.

I have little doubt that their more gifted soldiers are waiting in the wings, ready to pour forward when the time comes. And though it may appear as though our defence is holding easily, and we're slowly wiping out their threat, I'm certain the truth is very different.

Morning fails to bring the usual illumination you'd expect. As dawn begins to rise, and the sun climbs, little light penetrates the shroud. The only real change is that the smoke and murk takes on a different shade, turning to a brighter grey from a colourless black. But it remains no less impenetrable, our vision still dulled by it, our eyes unable to work through it.

And I begin to consider that, perhaps, I was right before. That the Cure have people capable of holding the shroud in place, keeping the city stifled by it, caught within its grip.

Are they out there right now, their Elementals, pressing the air into the city, forcing the smoke to sit firm? Do they have them set around our flanks, surrounding us, creating this trap from which we cannot escape?

As the bouts of fighting take a hiatus during the early morning, I ask Zander that very thing. He doesn't have an answer for me, but seems to agree it could be the case.

"Then we should get out there," I tell him. "Form strike teams…use this fog against them. If we can't see them, then they won't be able to see us either. We can use it to our advantage."

"I don't know, Brie," he says wearily as we stand in the control room beside the southern gate, soldiers still rushing about around us. "We have no real idea of what's going on out there. It's too dangerous."

I grimace, my head pounding hard from the constant noise.

"I swear, Zander, I'd go out there myself to try to destroy whatever damn machine is making that bloody sound! I can't stand it anymore. We should get out there and blow them up if nothing else…"

"Trust me, the thought's gone through my mind several times already. But I reckon that's exactly what they want. It's a lure, sis. They want us to go and sabotage these machines so they can take us down when we're out there and vulnerable. We've got to think several steps ahead of them."

"Or maybe you're just giving them too much credit," I say, not believing my own words.

"After what they've done, I think they deserve the credit. We can't underestimate them. We can't leave the city walls."

He puts to bed my fledgling plan, basic and poorly thought out as it was. I'd actually thought a little bit further ahead; my idea would be grab some of their corpses from beyond the wall, dress up as them, and then sneak out in disguise. We could then take out their damn sonic machines, and maybe find out if they do have some Elementals keeping this smog among the streets.

A simple plan, and probably a desperate one based off of a lack of sleep, piercing headache, and growing fear that we're just sitting ducks here. We have to be proactive. We have to strike back. We can't, as far as I see it, just wait here as they pepper our walls and try to break down our doors. Eventually, they will. And when that happens…who knows.

In fact, part of me is looking forward to that very thing. As soon as they crack the egg, the yolk will have no choice but to come oozing out. We will need to fight them head on, battle them man for man. They'll head straight for the breach and will come surging through the bottleneck. It might just be a good chance to kill some of the bastards as they try to get in.

With the morning now in full flow, I get no chance to sleep or rest. None of us do. We have to stay vigilant, always forced to go to where the fighting seems most vicious, to the points of the wall thought most at threat.

They don't let up. They don't let us rest. They come, again and again, in waves, attacking and retreating, then attacking somewhere else. All over the wall now, from the north to south and west to east, at least five to ten small skirmishes are constantly at play. And while they're able to retreat and pass the baton onto another of their units, we have no choice but to stay alert to stay alive.

Slowly but surely, they're seeking to wear us down.

CHAPTER NINETEEN

It isn't until mid-afternoon that I finally give in. Zander realises that I'm out on my feet and orders for me to rest.

"We've got it in order," he says. "Move back from the front line for a few hours. There's nothing to suggest they're going to break through for a while yet."

I feign some argument until I realise I don't even have the energy for that. Leaving Zander near the southern gate where he's running the show, I head back to the inner districts to a place I know quite well. Not far, in fact, from the very place where my part in all this started.

A little north of here, the once vibrant square of Culture Corner sits, lonely and abandoned, forgotten at this time of war. That terrorist attack by the Fanatics set me on this path, and how quickly I've travelled it to where I am now.

But it's not to Culture Corner that I go, but a cream building with fancy balconies and a wonderful array of colourful and sweet-smelling flowers adoring its façade. Only, that's how it once looked at least.

Now, the training school for girls seeking to

'marry up' to Inner Haven is a shadow of its former self. It doesn't lie in ruin like so many buildings in nearby streets, and doesn't appear to have suffered much in the way of structural damage. Yet the flowers are dead, and the balconies are covered in soot, and the outside isn't cream anymore and bathed in warm sunshine, but hidden in the murk of smoke that swallows the entire city.

I came here once, and marvelled at the place's opulence. Now, I merely take it for the refuge it has become, a place now housing the several hundred Fangs who fled here from the woods. And outside, guarding the doors and ever watchful, I see several of their hunters now, cloaked within the shroud and waiting for their chance to fight.

I step out of the car, brought here by a soldier who will now quickly return to the gate, and approach to find that one of the guards is, in fact, West. He takes a moment to recognise me before forgetting himself and stepping towards me energetically.

"Brie...what are you doing here?!" he asks.

The other few hunters drape an eye over him, still unused to hearing him speak. It appears that scene back in the central hut of their village, when he confronted and killed the envoy, has cast his muteness aside. In these final few days of life, he must feel it's time to say his piece.

"I came to check up on you all," I say. "And...to get some rest."

"Yes, of course. You look tired. Come, come, follow me."

I smile at the other guards, a couple of whom I recognise, and step into the building. The interior isn't how I remember it either. It has a coating of mud and filth that has clearly been traipsed in by the Fangs, wandering in and out from the streets and bringing the grime with them. The air is cleaner than outside, but still stuffy and smoky, and there's a constant hum of voices and movement coming from all corners.

Just peeking through a few doors, I can see that all available space is taken. The Fangs huddle together, most likely hating being inside such a structure, and wondering just why they're here when the city is under bombardment. Perhaps they'd have been better heading north to the Roosters after all, or else migrating away from these lands for good.

That chance has gone now. They're part of this just like the rest of us.

As West leads me through the hall, I hear a familiar voice. While the sweet smell of flowers may be absent, that of Sophie's voice still remains. Exiting from a room, she hustles her way past us before realising it's me. Then she turns, shakes her head to herself, and snatches me into an embrace.

"Oh Brie, you look a fright. What are you doing here? How is the defence going? Have you seen much of Rycard?"

The questions flow, as expected. I assume that, back here away from the fighting, Sophie and the Fangs are being kept largely out of the loop.

I answer the most important query first.

"Rycard's fine, Soph," I say. "He's over by the western gate last I heard, helping out Commander Burns."

"Oh…the western gate?" she asks, eyes narrowing in worry. "Isn't that where most of the fighting is?"

"Um, I'm afraid the fighting's pretty well dispersed. We've, erm, got it all in order," I say, nodding comfortingly.

Sophie isn't the woman she once was. Her naivety and innocence that I occasionally found grating have gone. She seems well aware that we're on the back foot here.

"That noise," she says, frowning. "That incessant noise. I assume it's to confuse us, stop the Bats from hearing properly?"

The battering of my eardrums isn't quite as bad back here. It's still endless and nauseating, but not to the same extent as around the perimeter.

"Yeah, exactly."

"And the smoke, that's to stop our Hawks from seeing?"

I nod.

"Tell me the truth, Brie. Are we really safe here?"

"Oh yeah, sure," I say brightly. "If you weren't, Rycard or someone would have sent the order to move you to Inner Haven…"

"No," she cuts in, "that's not what I mean. I mean, all of us? Are we all safe here, in the city?"

She looks at me with a flat gaze that doesn't call for lies. West's face is a little more innocent, though there's a fire behind his eyes that still bids for further vengeance against the band that murdered his people.

"I don't know," I answer after a moment. "This smoke, this noise…we couldn't plan for that. But they've played their hand now. I can't imagine that they've got many more tricks up their sleeve."

Sophie nods quickly, and smiles, her old self flashing.

"So, did you come here to tell us that?"

"Erm, I guess, partly. But mainly to get some rest. Zander ordered it."

"Yes, you look like you need it. How about you take my bed. I'll be sure to wake you if anything happens."

"I was gonna say. Thanks, Sophie."

"OK, this way, darling."

I'm led up the stairs and onto the landing, West coming along for the ride as if keen to complete his escort until I'm nicely settled. Sophie's room, at the end of the corridor, is no longer just for her. There are a number of beds and mattresses there, apparently used by the other women tasked with managing the Fangs.

"That one's mine," she says, pointing to a proper bed, pushed up against the wall in the far corner. "So, Zander knows you're here? I assume he'll radio us if he needs you?"

"I assume so," I say tiredly, although do wonder if this is my brother's way of pushing me back from the fight and keeping me from harm's way. Old habits die hard, after all.

Sophie looks to West.

"Um, West…come now, let's leave Brie to get her rest."

West nods and smiles shyly at me, before slipping from the room.

"So, I'll wake you in, what, three hours?" asks Sophie.

"Make it two," I say. "I need to get back as soon as possible."

"Two it is."

She smiles, shuts the door, and leaves me in silence. Or, at least, the best approximation of silence given the interminable wailing. I move straight for her bed and sit down, hardly realising that I'm sprinkling soot all over the sheets. I lie down, slowly, and shut my eyes, my mind flashing with images and ears still throbbing hard.

I could do with a pill to help me sleep, or else one to stave off this headache. Or better yet, I could do with having Adryan here, tucked up behind me, arm over my waist, breath warming the back of my neck.

I wonder, even though I'm only a couple of miles away from him right now, whether I'll ever see him again. Will I ever see Brenda and Tess? Will I see my grandmother again? Or little Abby? Or even Drum, perhaps only a few streets away with his unit.

Who knows, maybe I'll never even see my twin brother again. Perhaps I'll drop off to sleep right now, and be shaken awake by Sophie to the news that the wall has been breached in the south. That the Cure have swarmed in like the plague of vermin they really are. That Zander, trying to defend the city, exhausted from the night's exertions, has fallen. And the rest of us are soon to follow.

I lie there with those thoughts in my head and all I want is to get back out there. I don't want to lie here, away from it all. I don't want to sleep and miss a beat. I want to die on my feet, fighting, and not wake to learn that the city has already fallen.

But what I want isn't relevant to the physical needs of my body. The thoughts flow consciously, before the curtain closes and I drop away into dreams and my mental wanderings are taken on by my subconscious mind instead. I only know that I've caught a bit of time behind my lids when I feel my body shaken, and my eyes crack open.

It isn't Sophie who stands above me, but a far different figure. The bearded, shaven headed form of Rhoth materialises from the silhouette as I blink several times, quickly working out just where I am and what's going on.

When I do, it comes in a flash. I sit straight up on the bed and ask, "What time is it?! How long was I out?"

"It's evening time," says Rhoth as the ceaseless wailing once more filters into my ears. "You have been asleep for several hours…"

"Several? I told Sophie only two."

"Several. Two. No difference. What matters is, do you feel better?"

"Yeah, better," I say, standing. "I need to get back."

"Yes, of course you do," says Rhoth. "Perhaps I come too, bring my hunters with me. We don't like sitting here, waiting for the fight to come to us."

"I fear you won't have to wait too long, Rhoth," I say. "Have you heard any developments from the front?"

"Nothing," he grunts. "No one tells us anything here. More gunfire and explosions…and that horrible sound. Been the same all night and day."

"OK, well I think you deserve to know," I say, drawing a smoky breath of air. "The Cure are testing for weaknesses in the wall and trying to exhaust us. This is worse than we thought it would be. They'll break through sooner or later, and most likely the former. Is it dark outside yet?"

"Dusk. Darkness is coming. Smoke is turning black again."

"Then it'll happen soon I think. You say you're not being told anything here. That's because the military are too busy defending the wall from all sides. You can't rely on them for information. I think…I *know* it's time for you to move back."

"Move back?" questions Rhoth. "No, we move forward to fight, not back."

I shake my head.

"No, you need to get your old and young to safety first. If the Cure breach the walls, it'll be too dangerous here. You need to get them behind the walls to Inner Haven. It's much safer there."

"They told us that the order would come for that when needed…"

"Yeah, I know. But they didn't expect all this. I'm making the decision myself. I'm giving the order myself. Get your people to the southern gate to Inner Haven. Then, if you and your hunters want to fight, feel free to join us…"

Rhoth begins to nod, and eyes me with a smile creasing across his lips. They peel back, revealing those fangs of his, filed sharp.

"The girl has become a soldier and warrior…and now a commander. You and your brother are so very alike."

I take it as a firm compliment, especially from Rhoth.

"Then you'll do as I say?"

"I will. If you think it's best, Brie, then I will escort my people to your inner city. But me and my hunters will not cower there. We will offer what help we can give. We will get revenge for all those lost."

I raise a hand, stretching it out to lay it on his shoulder.

"I'd expect nothing less from you, mighty Rhoth."

Together, we head down the stairs to spread the word. Rhoth begins updating his people on the plan, and I hunt down Sophie to update her too.

"Oh, thank goodness," she says. "I was hoping for the order to come through. Who gave it? Rycard? I didn't realise you had a radio on you…"

She inspects my clothes with a frown.

"No radio, Soph," I say. "The order, well…the order has come from me. I've got a feeling that you won't be safe here for long. Better to get to safety now while you can."

"Right, yes…of course. We all trust you, Brie. I'll make arrangements immediately."

"Good. Do you have vehicles here?"

"No. Well, just a couple of cars. Not enough to transport the people."

"Right, go on foot. There's time. But, if you could drive me back to the front first, that would be useful. I'd rather get there as quickly as possible."

"Of course, Brie. I have my car. No trouble. Just give me a few moments to update the girls."

"Sure, I'll be outside."

I move through the building, passing Rhoth again on the way.

"I'm heading back, Rhoth. I'll see you again, I'm sure."

"Yes, we will see each other, Brie. Good luck."

"And to you."

I leave him to organise his people and move back onto the street. West is absent this time, other Fangs now on duty. Immediately, the wailing grows louder, and I see that the light is fading once more, darkening the swamp of smoke.

And within the growing gloom, I feel a sense of urgency fill me. Tonight, I know, I won't be getting any more sleep...

CHAPTER TWENTY

Sophie's car isn't the same one she used to drive. Because, well, that one she didn't have to drive at all. As a driverless vehicle, we never had to do anything but sit in the back and be chauffeured where we wanted on command. Now, however, the car she's been given requires a little more manual input.

It's immediately obvious to me that she has little experience behind the wheel. Even though the vehicle is automatic and doesn't require complicated gear changes, she still has some trouble navigating us down the streets, driving rather more slowly than I'd like and nervously taking us around any debris blocking our path.

We work our way further south towards the wall, the beating drums of war still sounding all over, and that incessant wailing growing more aggressive the closer to the ramparts we get.

"I don't know how you can bear it at the front line," she says, wincing at the sound. "I can barely hear myself think."

"Exactly. These so-called barbarians are smart. You don't have to take me right to the front, don't worry, Soph. Drop me a few blocks back and then get to Inner Haven as quick as you can with the Fangs."

"Are you sure? I can go to the gate if you want?"

The brittle nature of her voice suggests it's an offer she'd prefer me not to accept. I don't. There's no need for her to venture right to the line, and in any case, there's someone I want to see on the way.

Several blocks back, Drum's unit is posted. He's part of a security cordon along one of the main roads heading inward, the likely path of any major assault should the Cure breach the walls nearby. Seeing as I'm passing close by, and this might be my last chance to see him, I'm not going to let the opportunity slip away.

I ask for Sophie to stop just before the cordon, and she does so without hesitation. I hug her tight and reiterate once more the need to get back to Inner Haven as soon as possible. She wishes me luck, probably quite aware than I'll need it, and shoots straight off before her façade can crack.

I watch her go for a moment, then turn my eyes on the large presence of soldiers up the street. They're well fortified, with a number of blockades in place, fixed machine gun positions, snipers on rooftops and in windows and drones hovering about in the sky.

Though visibility remains poor, it's not quite as bad here as at the wall. I imagine the snipers can see further, and any potential attacks this way won't be quite such a surprise. The drones, too, will be quite capable of signalling alarms to present some warning. Hopefully the same is true throughout Outer Haven, the many major streets well watched and marshalled.

I head for the force of soldiers, at least two or three hundred of them stationed here, with the capability of defending adjoining streets if necessary. A good proportion of them appear to be Con-Cops, but there are many garbed in the dark armour of the City Guards too, and a number of Nameless soldiers sprinkled in among them.

There might even be a hybrid or two, or perhaps a couple of Stalkers here. Mostly, I know our most powerful soldiers are on the front line, but major intersections like this also require a great deal of protection. It's to these battlements that our men will fall back if required to. The standing army here will, therefore, be significantly bolstered when the time comes.

It's a member of the City Guard who commands this force, and I see him as I approach, chatting down the radio in a little field camp off to one side. I choose not to disturb him, but search immediately for Drum, his size usually enough to point him out from the crowd.

Today, with the air being so smoky, that isn't so easy. And unusually, Drum isn't the largest person here. I spot several other towering figures, massive Brutes with their exoskeleton armour, fixed with miniguns and other potent firearms. Drum certainly won't be kitted out the same. Compared to them, he's rather small, and certainly isn't experienced enough to be trusted with such weaponry.

Instead, I find him towards the rear, watching a side-street with several other men. They sit behind metal shelters, capable of withstanding most types of ballistics, little to do but wait for the war to come to them.

I approach Drum through the fog, and this time refuse to treat him as a soldier. Instead, I treat him as the dear friend he is, the adopted younger brother he is, and wrap my arms straight around his massive trunk before he can deny me. I feel his strong arms rest gently against my back, before his grip slowly grows stronger.

"Are you OK?" I ask weakly.

I draw away from him and look up into his big face. I still hate seeing him here, with this patchwork of armour on his body, and this rifle in his arms. Drum is too gentle for this life. He should be back at Compton's Hall with the others…

But then, that's the old Drum. He's changed now, and I have to accept that. What sort of a man would he be if he were hiding there with the kids, and not out here, ready to protect them? No, that wouldn't suit him at all. Whether I like it or not, he's best served out here, putting himself on the line like so many others, even those of his same callow years.

His answer, when it comes, isn't verbal. He merely frowns a little, as if the other solders are watching, and then nods. Only after I've let him go does he grunt, "I'm good."

"Rested? Did you get any sleep?"

"Some," he admits. "We've been taking watches."

I don't tell him that doing so is sort of pointless right now. Until the enemy get into the city, there's nothing to watch out for. Then again, what the hell do I know? This is just as new for me as it is for him. I may have some useful powers and gifts, but I hardly know what I'm talking about when it comes to battle tactics and soldiery.

In fact, I'm fairly certain that, while I worry about Drum, he probably does the same for me. I'm only a couple of years older than him, after all. I guess I forget that sometimes...

"You heading back to the wall?" he asks me.

I nod.

"I need to stay near Zander."

"Right, of course. Be careful out there, Brie. It seems like the fighting's getting more intense. I don't think the wall will be able to hold out much longer."

"It won't," I admit.

"And we're not sending soldiers out to stop them?"

"We can't, Drum. Zander says it's too dangerous. I saw what they could do in the woods. We have to make our stand here."

Drum nods his great head, his solid chin, sprouting the odd hair, dipping up and down.

"I suppose we have no choice. Some of the men want to get out there and fight, though. When the battle comes here, we'll be ready. We want them to come here. We dare them."

"Good attitude," I say, smiling. Not condescendingly. No, I'm done with that. Just supportively. "We all need to do our bit."

Even you...

I don't linger much longer. Hugging Drum again, once more against his will, though more briefly this time, I leave him without any further words. Only a smile is needed, and a glint in the eye to tell him unequivocally that we're going to win this damn thing.

Then, slipping back into the fog, I head off down the street, only looking back once I've turned a corner. I look to see Drum retaking his position, vigilant in his task as he gazes off down the street, ready and waiting to do his part.

"Goodbye, Drum," I whisper, blinking a burgeoning tear from my eye. "Please be safe."

Then, with that final look, I twist and dash away, setting my mind back on my brother. I rush through the security cordon and up the street, drawing the eyes of all soldiers in the area, and feel the atmosphere of dread that fills the air.

Yet that dread is suffocated by another emotion. Anger. A fury that flows through the blood of all the assembled men and women. A collective hate for those who come to kill us, and our friends, and our families.

It is a powerful emotion indeed, and one that

serves us all well. When you need that extra push, that extra ten per cent in the fight, anger and hatred will often supply it.

And while this army of the Cure comes to pillage and destroy, we are here to protect and defend. And that, too, is a more powerful motivator.

So through I go, rushing on, my presence helping to inspire in a manner similar to my brother. Some will look at me and see him, their young commander who has accomplished so much, who has such great power within his veins. Yet others will be inspired by me, for me alone. For the things I can do too, and the whirlwind my life has become.

From normal cleaner girl, just an orphan in Outer Haven, I have become a leading figure in this city. A shining light for others to follow. My story is one of triumph against adversity, a girl rising to meet her destiny.

And tonight, perhaps, that destiny will unfold. Will I die, along with everyone else? Will I live, and see others I love fall?

I do not know. I can't know.

Only time will reveal my path.

CHAPTER TWENTY ONE

As I rush the few remaining blocks towards the southern gate, passing by crippled buildings and through war-torn streets, the sound of wailing, gunfire, and explosions grows ever louder.

With the sky beyond the smog now turning dark once again, the lights of the pulse rifles, spitting in the distance, begin to grow clear. Reds and blues and greens collaborate to paint a haunting and yet beautiful picture as I move swiftly to the wall. They colour the smoke and join together, forming other hues within the mist that seems to contrast so strikingly with the booming sounds of war.

Death, it seems, can be beautiful. War is nothing but a brutal symphony.

When I finally reach the gate, I'm quick to march straight for the control room. I find it as I left it, filled with soldiers zipping here and there, the war effort down here along the southern perimeter coordinated from this room.

And over in the west, it will be Commander Burns and Rycard leading the charge. And in the north, that role will be taken by Colonel Hatcher. Here, however, it is Zander who commands our men, liaising constantly with the other leaders dotting the city as he bids to ensure our defence holds.

I charge straight for him, desperate to hear any updates.

His eyes craft their way up to mine, identical. Though mine are now well rested, and his are bloodshot and intense. It appears that my brother hasn't had any sleep at all. A man in his position cannot afford such a luxury.

"What's been happening?" I ask hurriedly, keenly aware that the pace appears to have quickened somewhat.

My brother's expression doesn't inspire a huge deal of confidence.

"They're wearing us down, sis," he says. "I'm not sure how much longer we can hold."

"Where? Where will they breach first?"

He shakes his head, pointing towards a monitor with a map of the city. His finger traces the wall in a number of different places.

"Here, here, here," he starts saying. "It won't take long before several areas collapse. We're trying to arrange our best soldiers to meet them when they do, but they keep moving around out there. We never know where they'll attack next."

"Then what? Station separate units at all weak points?"

He nods.

"We have standing forces at each potential breach, with other mobile units ready to move right there as soon as the order comes. How…how did you sleep? Are you rested, Brie?"

"I'm fine, yeah. I take it you haven't had a chance?"

He shakes his head.

"Well, what about now? Get a few winks?"

I know the suggestion is ridiculous. He can't possibly leave the line now. He'll have to make do.

"It's too late for that. I feel strong. Adrenaline will keep me going for some time yet. How did you get back here?""

"Sophie drove me most of the way. I stopped at the main blockade towards the north."

"Right, right. I've been in contact with them. They're ready for the fight when it comes their way."

"That's the impression I got. Oh, I should tell you, I ordered Sophie and the Fangs to head to Inner Haven. I had a feeling time was short, and I didn't want them forgotten."

Zander's eyes shape in a fashion that suggests they had indeed slipped his mind. Though, I suspect the likes of Rycard would have made sure his wife was alerted and sent to the safe zones.

"Good. And Rhoth, how did he take it?"

"Pretty well. I told him he should get them to safety, then come on out and join the fight once he's done. I'm guessing we might need all the help we can get out here."

"Yeah, you're probably right. But that's part of the problem – this is still just a guessing game. We won't know how capable their entire army is until we get them fighting in the streets."

"We had them on the ropes in the woods until those Elementals came along," I remind him. "And there's no way the rest of the army will be as incisive as that lot."

"No, they won't. But neither are our soldiers. Half our ranks are filled with Con-Cops. They're not the greatest soldiers."

"Nope, but they're fearless and remorseless. Not the worst people to have on your side."

I don't allow myself to think about who they really are. Behind their masks, somewhere hidden in their minds, are normal, good people. It's only their reconditioning that's made them as they are, and we know who to blame for that…

"You're right," says Zander. "Now lets…"

He doesn't get to complete his sentence. A sudden flurry of action sounds behind us, and we swivel to find a soldier calling us over. We hurry to his side, and find him hovering over a screen showing footage from one of our few security drones still creeping around beyond the wall.

"Sir, it looks like a big attack is incoming," says the man tensely.

He's right. On the monitor, a great mass of soldiers seems to be moving through the mist. It's a formless silhouette, but the impression is very clear.

There are hundreds of them, and heading right for the wall.

"Where is that?" questions Zander fiercely.

The soldier points to a larger monitor, hand steady.

"There, sir. To the west of here, half a mile."

Zander peers in.

"It's a weak point," he says. "We have a force there, but not a big one. Send a mobile unit instantly. Inform them I'm on my way."

The soldier nods, and Zander sweeps off out of the room with me rushing in his wake. Outside, the area around the gate is more hectic than ever, a number of wounded now being brought down from various positions along the wall and many of the vehicles used for transporting our forces absent or haphazardly parked.

We head straight for Zander's jeep and jump inside, and off down the street I see one of our mobile infantry convoys shooting off west along the southern perimeter. Zander hits the gas as we quickly zoom after them, pressing through the thick mist and heading straight for the wall a little under a thousand metres away.

When the wall comes into view once more, I notice that it's an area with less fortifications and barricades, and from what I can see, no large gun placements whatsoever. The standing force here isn't large – a hundred or less soldiers – but along with the influx of the mobile unit, that number is quickly doubled.

Up on the wall, our soldiers wait, and as we step out of the car, Zander quickly commands for others to join them. We go too, moving for the stairs and climbing. It's clear enough, even through the smoke, that the wall has suffered some major damage, smouldering in places and with its façade threatening to crumble.

"Quickly, quickly," hisses Zander, urging us into position.

We move quietly, though probably don't need to due to the din, keeping low behind the metal barriers that shield the top of the wall. Several dozen soldiers, most of them highly capable, fix in position and wait. I stay low as Zander peers through the narrow window in the barrier, seeking out the enemy as they creep towards the wall a little off to our right.

"I see them," he whispers. "Fifty metres out." His eyes shift right and left. "Prepare to fire, on my signal."

He doesn't give the signal immediately. All soldiers along the line ready their weapons, pointing the barrels of their pulse rifles through the small windows in the barrier and aiming them right at the incoming soldiers. I stand a little taller and do the same, and through the fog the enemy comes into view.

It's hard to determine how many there are. They're well dispersed, most barely visible in the smog. I can see several dozen of them at the front, though those behind remain hidden. The monitor suggested there were hundreds. I have no reason now to refute that supposition.

I feel a knot begin to tie up my insides, and the endless wailing appears to quieten slightly in my head. I wait for my brother to call out and start firing, but he still holds firm, perhaps wishing for the entire force to get a little closer before he lets loose the fire.

Then, suddenly, the soldiers stop. Still, only a smattering of them are visible, blurred shapes that occasionally grow clearer as the smoke is pressed away by a sudden breeze, before accumulating and falling once more. It seems to thicken more than ever, a cloud gathering right ahead of us along this specific stretch of wall.

Is there an Elemental out there, just beyond our sight? Is he forming this cloud to hide the attack?

"We should fire," I whisper harshly, looking to Zander.

A temptation runs through me, calling for me to do so and begin the inevitable avalanche. Zander's cool words halt my thinking.

"Not yet...we need to know what we're firing at."

Here, there are no large guns protecting us. With only so many available, they had to be dispersed in a way to try to protect all parts of the wall. Yet, some stretches were always going to be more vulnerable. That was unavoidable. And here, at this particular point, the only guns are a little to the west and east, a little too far to join the fight. And right now, they're firing elsewhere, their own battles to contend with.

We are very much alone.

And the enemy know it.

I continue to watch as the front-line soldiers of the Cure begin to disappear into the growing mist. And as they do, a slight rumble seems to vibrate through the earth. I feel it through my boots, the wall beneath my feet shivering as though caught in a stiff breeze. And the air, too, seems to hum and buzz.

The soldiers down the line share glances. I do the same with my brother, but find his eyes staring forward, narrowing. The rumbling grows a little more intense, the foundations of the walls shaking harder, and the source of the energy begins to grow clear.

It's from behind the soldiers just ahead of us. Somewhere behind them, within the shroud, a great power is stirring. Setting my finger tighter to my trigger, I begin to pull down, ready to fire. And as I do, I see the barely visible soldiers ahead start to part, moving swiftly left and right and creating a gap in their line.

It happens fast, and before I know it the trembling is building to a crescendo, and through the gap shapes come flying.

Between the men they come, dark forms of varying sizes and shapes. I use my Dasher powers to try to slow my perception of the world, and zoom in with my Hawk eyes to see that they're mostly trunks of trees, burnt to a crisp and ripped from the earth. The remains of the scorched woodland, thick hunks of wood torn from their foundations in the ground and thrust towards the wall at a tremendous pace.

Other shapes comes too. I see bits of rock and stone, blackened by the fire and taken from their homes in the outerlands. They join the trunks of trees and head straight for the wall, battering it hard, smashing it into submission.

And mingled in with the wood and rock, I even see flesh; the bodies of dead soldiers from the Cure's army, now drawn up from the battlefield and hurled right at us along with the rest.

The sight is enough to cause a brief paralysis to flow down the line, our soldiers gaping at the show of power, disbelieving. Beyond the smoke that now hides them, back from the line, an Elemental of great strength can be the only culprit. Perhaps more than one, standing together combining their gifts to raise such objects from the ground and send them crashing into the city's faltering façade.

The attack comes so suddenly and with such ferocity that we don't react immediately. Even Zander appears bowed by the display, and takes a moment to realise he has no choice now but to order our attack.

Over the din, he does so. His voice suddenly scrapes from his worn-out throat, and along with it his pulse rifle begins to spit blue flame down into the smog beyond the top of the wall. Mere moments later, the rest of us join him, and a hundred rifles begin roaring their response.

The smoky cloud lights up like a rainbow once more, and I search through the illumination to see the soldiers of the Cure drawing forward shields to protect them. They're rudimentary, but just enough to hold back the flame for now, our fire directed to all parts but tending to seek out those we see.

Zander's voice rips through the noise once more.

"Fire at the Elemental," he calls out. "Kill him!"

We can't see him, or them, but know where they must be. From the mist, where the trunks of trees and rocks, and dead bodies come, we begin to aim our guns. All red and blue and green flame now begins to gather to one point, setting trunks and corpses alight as they come, the wall now peppered with flaming debris as well.

But the bombardment doesn't stop. And soon I see just why.

Through the mist, a single Elemental comes. Not two or more. Just one. One man, imbued with terrible power similar to those I saw when Kira was taken from us. But this man isn't the same. These soldiers aren't the same. This army isn't the same.

He comes, arms aloft and still drawing up all nearby debris for the assault. But he has a shield too, metal barriers hovering around him, held up by his ability to control such things with his mind. They cover him from head to toe, and I only see him through a slight gap as he moves. And around him, other soldiers stand with their own shields, offering greater protection to this man with such power.

"Shoot him!" shouts Zander. "Kill him!"

The desperation in his voice is deep, sending shudders through me. We all fire right in his direction, but nothing seems to get through. And still, over to our right, the section of the wall under attack continues to weaken, and the men who stand atop it flee off to the flanks to escape the barrage.

There is no respite, and there seems nothing we can do. It only lasts a minute or two, but it's all this Elemental needs. Pressing the final debris at the wall, still hidden behind his shields, the barrage seems to end with the wall still standing.

I wonder, for the briefest of moments, whether we've done enough. Whether the wall is more than he can handle, too thick and strong to be downed by such missiles.

How wrong I am.

He has another trick to deploy.

With our pulse rifles still firing, clattering hard into the shields around him and partially held back by his staggering powers, a sudden lull falls as the vibrations stop. But they don't stop for long. The lull lasts a split second, the rumbling halted before brewing once again in a more terrible fashion than ever.

It builds and builds for several seconds before, suddenly, a pulse of energy flows through the earth, emitted from the man's body, his mind. It carves a path through the ground, ripping it up, before reaching the wall and doing the same.

The weakening stone and metal construct can take no more. It bursts apart, split down the middle and sending shards of itself left and right and high into the air. I watch in horror as it's breached, exploding before my eyes and creating a gap big enough for the soldiers to pour through.

I look at Zander, whose eyes are no longer weary. They're bright, tense, and fearful just like mine.

The city has been cracked open.

And turning his eyes down to the soldiers behind the wall, awaiting this exact event, he shouts out.

"Hold the line! Protect the breach!"

CHAPTER TWENTY TWO

This stage of the fighting was always going to come. The city was never likely to hold out forever, not after what we'd seen. Once, perhaps, when they first marched to our doors, we considered them a threat that could be repelled without too much difficulty.

Now, it is clear enough that we are all in a fight for our lives.

If they can breach the walls of Outer Haven, then there's no reason why they can't do the same to Inner Haven. We have to stop them before they get there. We have to battle them in the streets. And the face-to-face combat that many of us have asked for is now set to begin.

And it starts right here in the south.

As the debris from the broken wall continues to fall, raining down from above, we fire at those who pour forwards from our precarious perch. And behind the broken wall, our men take their positions, launching their flame at the bottleneck, hoping to catch as many of the enemy in the growing inferno as possible.

It all happens so fast, and our attention seems to be taken by the soldiers now set to enter the city.

For that split second, the Elemental is forgotten. He's remembered quickly when another pulse of energy rips from where he stands, galloping towards the wall once again and opening the gap much wider.

More rock and stone hurtles into the sky, and I see a number of our soldiers, manning the wall, going right along with it. They spiral skyward before coming back down and disappearing into the smog, and as the rain of debris sprinkles the streets, the enemy begin to flow.

I see them now, all of them rushing forward at extraordinary speed. All Dashers and heaven knows what else, they rush for the gap and slide into cover behind, shooting at our men and displacing, trying to get beyond our cordon, flank it, destabilise it so more of them can pour forward.

I fire from above, shooting at the gap through the soot and dust, until I feel Zander's hand come down on my shoulder, twisting me around as he shouts, "MOVE!"

He draws me back just in time as I see the Elemental preparing another shockwave, and we retreat along with our soldiers as it rushes for the wall just right of where we stand. Once more, the ramparts explode, the gap widening, our defence weakening.

We have no choice now but to descend and join the battle below. We gallop for the stairs, firing as we go, and I notice that the Elemental is now retreating, sinking back into the shadows, his job done.

I wonder if he's their leader, or one of them at least? Or just a soldier, thought too valuable to waste now in a direct attack. Or maybe, just like our Dasher powers, his energy can be depleted, and he requires some time to rest. I dearly hope the latter is the case. Such power can turn a war.

From the top of the wall, we move to the bottom, and begin setting our eyes to the breach where the enemy pour through. It's large now, at least thirty metres wide, the surrounding space filling with broken shards of stone and rock that offer cover as the Cure come forward.

All over, a little way back from the wall, our soldiers hide. They fire from behind the barricades set up here, the smoke still so thick it's hard to see who's who. The armour and garb of the Cure is different from our own, particularly the official uniforms worn by the Con-Cops, City Guards, and Stalkers who all have their own distinctive outfits.

It is more like the clothing worn by the rebels, the Nameless, random patchworks of armour and combat gear. And through the smoke, it remains difficult determining just who might be who, a problem that will no doubt increase when the fighting spreads beyond the breach.

Yet here we make our first stand, controlling the areas just beyond the wall and refusing to let the enemy come through. As I add my weapon to the fray, Zander immediately gets onto the radio, calling for more mobile units to advance to our position.

Before long, he knows, with more of the enemy spreading to this point, we will be overrun.

His conversation is hidden to my ears by the deafening soundtrack of war. The wailing from beyond the city now barely registers, hundreds of weapons firing at much closer proximity to where I make my stand. From our side, pulse rifles fizz and hiss. On theirs, chattering gunfire from rifles and handguns cackles into the air.

What seems to start as a short stalemate quickly morphs. Using the shroud for cover, their Dashers slip quickly closer, and our own are forced to fight them head on. It appears as though they have no fear, rushing forward and trying to overwhelm us. It's as if they know that more of our soldiers will be quickly arriving, and need to clear a path for their people to enter before that time comes.

Yet we hold our lines as best we can, a good number of hybrids and Stalkers among our defence. They use their own gifts well, taking down the weaker soldiers that come our way with ease, battling those with greater power on a more even level.

From my position, I see them cut down as they come, men dropping into the dust and consumed by the smoke. I'm responsible for several myself, the wall of fire sent from our soldiers' weapons so difficult to penetrate.

It seems they're prepared to sacrifice men in their pursuit of getting through. I'm reminded of the Con-Cops as they rush, fearing nothing, perhaps conditioned to fight without any concern for their lives. They rush in great numbers, and are killed in great numbers, but I suspect these people are little more than cannon fodder, sent in first to distract us as their more potent warriors work their way forward.

And so it happens. As we fire at the waves of soldiers, many of them zip here and there and quickly hunt down our positions. They shoot with heavy ballistics, explosive rounds now clattering into our cover and ripping our barricades apart. Our support isn't yet here. But theirs continues to come.

I know that we'll soon be overwhelmed, that our defence of the breach is about to end.

And so does Zander.

With loud calls rushing to our men, we begin to displace and move back. Some hear, others don't, voices hidden among the din. Hand signals are given too, but through the smog they're not always seen. Only the clear sign of Zander retreating into the streets indicates to any of us who see that we can no longer hold the opening in the wall.

So we move, withdrawing once more. Displacing to the north, we begin working our way to the next major cordon, stopping and firing and engaging when necessary. It's unordered chaos, our men struggling to hold back the tide and soon beginning to get lost within the smog. This endless cloud that refuses to leave. This mist that may be our undoing.

From my vantage at Zander's side, I have little idea as to the scope of what's going on. I see many of the enemy fall, dozens of them quickly killed as they come. And some of our men go the same way, the weaker among us caught out as we move back.

Yet the bigger picture is so hard to see. I can only do my part, dodging incoming gunfire and retaliating with interest, spreading north with our soldiers towards the nearest set of barricades.

Only when we have a short chance to stop, defending a new position deeper into the city, do I learn that our breach wasn't the only one.

From the radio, Zander learns the news and quickly passes it on.

"Two other breaches," he says. "In the northwest and over in the east. We're getting reports of more Elementals doing the damage. They're spreading in from three sides now."

"What do we do? Fall right back to Inner Haven? Defend the walls there instead?"

"No. We defend the streets here. We make our stand here."

The fighting that follows is hectic. My mind is only able to focus on the single task of killing anyone who comes my way, and trying my best to survive at the same time. My gifts as a Hawk allow me to see the incoming men early, and my Dasher powers are enough to help me avoid some shards of shrapnel and violent barrages of gunfire before they drench my position in deadly rain.

But I've never experienced anything like this. The attacks are continuous, aggressive, and seem to come from all sides. As we take position within a security blockade, joining the ranks of a number of our soldiers, we find ourselves quickly on the back foot once more.

They come down the main street ahead like locusts, swarming from the shroud. And calls come from our flanks, telling of smaller attacks through side-streets, our enemy creeping down quiet alleys that we don't have the manpower to defend.

I consider it madness to try to hold them here, in a city so vast. We need to move further to the centre where it's easier to defend, where the fighting isn't so spread out. Tighten up our defences, and there will surely be fewer gaps? Right now, it seems inevitable that they'll be able to work through places we cannot see, move inward towards Inner Haven without so much as a gun to call them to stop.

But my opinion counts for nothing here. Our senior commanders and skilled tacticians have designed our defence to fight them off before they reach Inner Haven. The various blockades around the city are considered the likely points of assault. All other avenues are watched by smaller contingents of men, and though some streets with be left unattended, all will eventually lead to the major roads through the city.

For all their planning, however, I doubt they expected this. Ever since the smoke came down, and the wailing began to call from beyond the walls, we've had our eyes and ears assaulted and neutered. We were put on the back foot, and have yet to begin striding forward.

The breaches were inevitable. The retreat was inevitable. And unless something drastic changes, it seems that an attack on Inner Haven will be inevitable as well.

As far as I see it, we have to attack to defend. Take out the sonic machines making all that racket. Kill the Elementals who seem to be holding this swamp of fog within the city.

Do that, and maybe we'll be able to fight them off. Do it not, and this night might just call an end to the city of Haven forever.

And that I cannot abide.

CHAPTER TWENTY THREE

I bring my request to Zander as we hold the enemy off at the blockade.

Not far to the northeast of here, along the main artery running between the southern gates of Outer and Inner Haven, Drum's own blockade is surely soon to be hit. And around the city, others are now deep into the fighting.

The word between our commanders is that we're holding strong for now. We can still displace to the inner blockades before resorting to moving straight for Inner Haven. The commands are simple: kill as many as we can before we have to move back. Reduce their numbers for the final assault, or else make them pay enough for them to have to withdraw.

As Zander continues to coordinate on the radio, I slip to his side and announce my plan.

"We need to organise small strike teams to move out beyond the walls," I start.

"Brie…not this again…"

"Zander! Listen to me. How long do you think we'll hold with this smoke and noise? It's destroying us. They clearly know how to fight in it, and we don't. It's giving them an advantage that's going to put us all in the ground…"

His eyes begin to change a little as I splutter. He seems to give me a moment longer to continue.

"They're in the city now, we can't stop that," I go on. "Before, maybe it was too dangerous going out there. But now, half their army is through the door, and the rest are still coming in. Now's our chance to strike out there before they reach Inner Haven. It might be our only chance."

He begins to nod, the roar of battle still raging around us.

"What do you have in mind?" he asks.

I recoil a touch at the query. He's really taking me seriously. I didn't expect that…

"Um, is Colonel Hatcher still alive?"

He nods.

"Right. He gets together a few of his best men and heads north. We do the same here and head south. We take out these sonic machines and kill their Elementals before they have another chance to strike. I still think there are some out there holding this smog in. And the ones who destroyed the walls must be recovering. They have to be weak. If we can kill them before they attack again, we turn the tables. For good."

He listens as I shout over the din. Then he asks, "And how do we get to the south? It's crawling down there. We might never make it…"

"The underlands," I say quickly, cutting him off. "You know them better than anyone. We go that way."

He shakes his head.

"They're mostly blocked. All tunnels are either buried from the fighting from before, or don't lead that way."

I'm thinking as he speaks, and a rather horrible thought comes to mind. But, it might just work. It might be perfect.

"The river," I say, fixing him with a firm glare. "The underground river takes you right beyond the city directly beyond the southern gate. There's no way they'll know about it. We'll come out in secret and strike at their heart. It'll work…I know it'll work."

I can see the concern already in his eyes. I'm fully aware that the plan is foolhardy at best, and downright suicidal at worst. But, then again, things have hardly been going our way recently. This might be our only shot.

"Right," he says nervously. "I guess the northern route through the underlands to the fields behind the church is still open. Colonel Hatcher could use that…"

"YES! Yes," I repeat, eyes bulging. "It's ideal, Zander. Seriously, let's do it. We can save the city!"

My enthusiasm surprises even me. It's not that I'm not afraid. I am. I'm terrified, in fact. It's more that I can't let them continue to come at us like this. I can't let them creep towards my friends in Inner Haven without doing everything I can to stop them, even if I die in the attempt.

Get rid of this smog, and shut down this damn wailing, and we'll take away their advantage. But above all, if we can get to their Elementals when they're weak, we have a shot.

A slim one, sure…but a shot nonetheless.

I wait a little longer for him to fully agree. He takes a bit more prodding, and I partially know why – Zander doesn't have a great fondness for water. From personal experience, I'm fully aware that the journey through the underground river is a perilous one in itself, and something I'd never, ever want to repeat. But, here I am, suggesting we go that way willingly. I guess that means I must be desperate.

"So…" I say, leaning in as we stay hidden beneath a barricade. "What do you say?"

I see the cogs turning behind his eyes, and even slip into his head to see the trickle of concerns building. Zander isn't reckless. He is a commander of soldiers and a fine strategist. Something like this, with so many things that might go wrong, isn't a choice he'd ever usually make.

Yet he knows, too, that it could pay off. That the risks are outweighed by the possible rewards. And that, right here, we will eventually be pushed back closer to the core of the city. Closer to the civilian population, hiding behind the walls of Inner Haven.

We're losing this fight right now, and he knows it.

Something needs to change.

I see it all behind his eyes, see him working through the possible outcomes. And though he still considers it foolhardy, he eventually decides to throw caution to the wind.

"OK," he says after some time. "I'll talk to Colonel Hatcher, tell him the plan. Wait here."

My lips shape into a beaming, determined smile, and I watch as he creeps down the line towards the radio. He takes possession of the line from another soldier, speaks hurriedly for a few minutes, and returns to my position. All the while, I stay low, only occasionally firing away down the street at the enemy but mostly watching Zander for his reaction.

When he reappears, he does so with his eyes aflame with purpose.

"Hatcher's holding the main street in the north. The best entrance to the underlands is a little south of where he is. He'll be able to get there without too much trouble."

"Great! So he's in?"

"He is. He's going to gather a couple of Stalkers and make for the north immediately. We have to do the same."

"Right. So who's going with us?"

"No one," he says. "This is a covert mission, and isn't about numbers. We'll be better suited going alone. And…if we die, I don't want too many of our best soldiers falling alongside us. We need to ensure the city is well defended."

I nod, no argument on my lips.

"Now come," he says, looking towards the north. "Let's get to it."

We begin retreating from the line, Zander informing the commander of the blockade of our plans. He seems somewhat distressed to lose us, but understands we have to go.

"Hold the line, commander," says Zander. "Spread the word across the city. We *must* hold the line."

The commander, a member of the City Guard, nods. He must be at least twice my brother's age, perhaps more, and yet appears happy to take orders from him. It speaks volumes to me of the man Zander has become, not just to the Nameless, but the others who flock to our collective cause.

With a final look, we press on northwards, hurrying away from the battle. As we go, the assault of constant gunfire lessens in my ears, and I'm able to get a better understanding of just how widespread the fighting has become. I can hear it now, ringing from where we came from, and from a little way to the east, and to the west as well. And all the way north, miles across the city, the faint sounds of battle reach my ears too.

The picture grows clear. All major routes towards Inner Haven are now fully engaged. All avenues towards the core of the city are being tested, just like the walls were, for weaknesses. And, just like with our perimeter defences, our toil will soon tell. It may take hours. It may take all night and the next day too. But eventually, the enemy will work their way inwards, and will begin to eat away at our heart.

That cannot be allowed to happen.

I can't let that happen.

As we continue north, heading closer to the inner districts of the southern quarter, we begin to hunt for a car. Convoys of our men rush past, heading now towards the fighting, going to where they're needed most. None can spare us the ride until we find one moving in the direction we wish to travel – to the western quarter not too far away, right towards the middle districts where the route to the underlands awaits.

It's a place I know well and once enjoyed. The beautiful underground cavern that held the waterfall and greenery, hidden away in the blackness that only my Hawk eyes could reveal. I used to enjoy going there when Zander first trained me. It was a place of peace and quiet, untouched by the city above.

Now, we're set to return, though I doubt I'll have time to stop and admire it.

Jumping into the back of a truck heading to help fortify the west, we move quicker now, unwilling to waste any energy we don't have to. The streets are clear and easy to navigate, and Zander, as he does, gives the soldiers we join a pep talk as we ride through the city, heading northwest from the south.

By the time we jump out, several blocks from our destination, the soldiers are buoyed and pumped and ready to go. We leave them as they continue on, pressing closer to the perimeter where they're needed, and once again find ourselves alone and in a part of the city that is still so dear to me.

It isn't as it once was, of course. District 5 was once my home, a bustling and busy and colourful world, now dead and empty. The smog hides most of it, but I know that beyond the smoke the giant screens are black and lifeless, and the buildings are cracked and broken, and the people who used to live here are absent, either dead or reconditioned or over in Inner Haven, cowering as the war creeps closer to their door.

So much has changed, and yet more change is yet to come unless we can stop it. A more dramatic change. A more profound change. A change that won't just alter the complexion of the streets, but will obliterate them entirely. That won't kill some of the people, but will rid this city of all who dwell here.

The thought fills me and keeps me going, all the motivation I, and all others defending the city, need. As the convoy moves west, Zander and I turn our attention towards the north, moving quickly now on foot through district 5 and towards district 6, right to the shelter that leads right down to the subterranean caverns beneath the city streets.

We rush, our bodies adorned in tightly fitted black armour and combat gear, pulse rifles fixed to our backs, belts with holsters and firearms and an array of grenades to deploy if we need to. We are a two-man team, hybrid twins, set to cut right into the heart of our enemy.

And like all soldiers who look upon my brother, I feel such strength by his side. It's as if my powers rise several notches when I'm near him. As if our minds, linked as one, allow us to operate as a single entity. The more time I spend with him, the more powerful I become. I can now sense what he's about to do before he does it. I can almost see what he sees, helping me get a far better perception of my surroundings.

I know he must feel the same. And though he always wishes to keep me safe and away from harm, maybe we're safest when we're together, watching each other's backs. Perhaps, as a duo, we'll one day become unstoppable.

If, that is, we live through the night.

So on we rush, galloping through district 5 and towards district 6, the fighting still chattering away from all directions in the distance. We come to a large intersection, and I know that straight towards the west is the gate out of the city. And that not too far away, one of our primary blockades in this quarter will be under heavy siege.

We step forward and make sure the coast is clear, before the rumbling of engines rises up in the air. I turn my eyes left and see a small convoy of two vehicles moving eastwards from the perimeter, heading, it would appear, towards Inner Haven.

It strikes me as odd for any of our soldiers to be going that way, away from the fighting, until I see that the vehicle belongs to a rather important figure.

"It's Director Cromwell's car," says Zander, spotting the vehicles as they come our way. "He must only just be heading for Inner Haven. Better late than never…"

"I guess Lady Orlando's got no option but to let him in," I grumble.

I have little time to further question it. Cromwell is the least of my worries right now.

Unfortunately, however, it seems he's about to jump right to the top of that list.

Neither of us see the event coming. Nor do the protective unit of Stalkers assigned to guard their master. As we stand there, waiting for the cars to pass before we move on, I spot movement from an alley on the other side of the road, just a little too late.

It all happens so fast that no one seems capable of reacting in time.

Explosive shells pour out from the smog, hitting the armoured cars and stopping them in their tracks. The vehicles screech and roll up onto their wheels, threatening to topple onto their sides. One does, hitting the ground and grinding towards the nearest building. The other teeters for a second before planting all four wheels back down and trying to continue on.

It doesn't get a chance. From the alley, a unit of enemy soldiers spread, well organised and moving like a highly trained military force. They move right for the two cars just as the doors open and the

Stalkers spill out, slightly disorientated, two of them shot down before they can even attempt to defend themselves.

I watch from the sides, hidden in shadow with my brother, as the carnage plays out. He makes a move to step into the light and join in, reaching around his back and setting his pulse rifle to his hands.

I hold him back.

"Brie, what are you doing? We need to help!" his voice clatters.

I look out again as the soldiers of the Cure engage with the Stalkers. The latter are now outnumbered, at least two to one. And two aren't engaging, because they have a very specific job to do – protect their master.

I see them down the street, pulling Director Cromwell from the overturned vehicle, hustling him towards the safety of a nearby building. Out on the streets, the ten or so enemy soldiers of the Cure press on, battling against the remaining four Stalkers. These particular Stalkers, I know, are highly proficient and assigned to Cromwell for that purpose. But the odds aren't in their favour, and all are under severe threat.

Zander makes a move to join once more. Once more, I grip him tight.

He shakes me off and grits his teeth.

"What the hell are you playing at?!"

I dart my eyes down the street.

"Let him die," I growl. "Cromwell…let him die. Let them all die, Zander."

His eyebrows drop into a frown so deep and severe I think he might just strike me where I stand. I counter with my own glare of conviction.

"Let him die right here," I say again. "Why should we save him?"

"Because if we don't," my brother reminds me, "all his Stalkers will stop fighting with us and start fighting against us! And all his Con-Cops too! You think we can let that happen right now?"

"And how do *know* that will happen? It could be lies. He can't have his Stalkers kill us if he's killed by the enemy…"

"We have no choice, Brie!" shouts Zander, cutting me off. He glares daggers at me. "Stay here if you want. I'm going."

He shoves my hand off him and sets his eyes down the street. Another Stalker has hit the dirt. One of the Cure is dead too. The odds haven't yet changed.

Until Zander steps in to join the fray.

CHAPTER TWENTY FOUR

For several long moments I don't engage. I merely stand there, frozen in place, finding it so hard to contemplate risking my own life to save Cromwell's.

As I see it, his little trick with the Stalkers and the Con-Cops might just be a veil. Maybe, if one of *us* were to kill him, then it would activate something in his men to attack us. But surely the same can't be the case for the enemy? Surely, if he were to die at the hands of one of the Cure, his soldiers wouldn't suddenly turn on us too?

He is, after all, committed to seeing the Savants, hiding over in Inner Haven, survive. How exactly would that cause be helped by his Stalkers and Con-Cops turning against us? Is he really so self-absorbed that he considers his own life above all others? That he's willing to let the entire city burn if his life is lost?

Because that's what will happen. If the Stalkers and Con-Cops suddenly swapped their allegiance, it would be game over for us all. The Cure would wipe us all out as we reignite our civil war, and the barbarian horde from the west would complete the job they came here to see through.

I have my doubts about whether that would happen, but like Zander said, right now we have no choice.

And while it sickens me to have to risk my life to save Cromwell's, I'd happily do it again and again in order to save my brother's. And right now, he needs me. Zander needs me.

So pulling the pulse rifle from my back, I look out at the battle and firm my jaw. It's time for me to engage.

I rush from my cover, dashing straight over to Zander who takes position behind the husk of an old car. Ahead, near the burning cars of Cromwell's convoy, the three remaining Stalkers do battle with what looks like eight enemy soldiers. And in the building nearby, Cromwell will be kept safe, covered by his two loyal guards.

My brother looks at me with a look that says, 'so you decided to join,' but spares no time to vocalise his thoughts. Instead, he stands from behind the vehicle and begins to spray his blue fire towards the enemy soldiers across the street. I do the same, and together we manage to take one of them out, his attention on the Stalkers and not us, his body quickly wreathed in cobalt flame and melting into the dirt.

Down the street, the three Stalkers seem to notice us. They glance with their dark eyes, and nod to show we're in this together. It's a slightly bizarre moment for me, even now after fighting alongside them for several days. I can only imagine how it must be for Zander.

The odds are now far better. Five of us against seven of them. With our pulse rifles set to their maximum potency, we fire once more into the smoke, destroying what cover the Cure are hiding behind. Our pulses of energy rip into old cars and the facades of buildings, tearing through brick and stone and metal alike.

It seems the enemy have little choice but to move. They zip away from our sight with tremendous speed, and I only just see them materialise again through the heavy smog. Two seem to come straight for my brother and me, whooshing forward and snatching knives from their belts, thinking their chances better in closer combat.

And down the street, the other soldiers do the same, pressing towards the three Stalkers, desperately trying to cut them down and fight their way towards Cromwell.

They must have come for him specifically. A special force, a powerful force, designed to sneak through our defences and hunt down the leader of the Savants. How they got word he was still here in Outer Haven, I cannot know. But really, it doesn't matter. They're here now, and Zander's right. We need to stop them from killing him.

I gather my wits just before the two soldiers arrive. Their faces show scars as they come, eyes filled with a manic hatred. One is large, the size of Rhoth, a powerful foe with speed to defy his mass. He heads straight for me, the smaller of the two men seeking out my brother. I can do nothing but step back as this shadow looms, drawing a long knife from his belt, rugged and nasty looking.

I suck a breath into my lungs and set my focus. My muscles hum and burn, and all my powers combine as my life comes under such direct threat. I can feel the same in my brother, and sense him about to launch a pre-emptive strike as his own foe comes calling. And I can sense, too, his concern for me, his desire only to cut down his enemy and come to my aid.

I don't want him to have to. I want to be able to stand against this man alone.

He's close now, metres away. He snarls, eyes wide and mad with a controlled fury. His knife-wielding hand appears like lightning and begins its journey towards me, ready to slash right through the weak point in both my armour and body, my neck partially exposed.

I know just where he's going to strike. I draw him forward and let him begin the motion, let him think I'm out of my depth. I'm not. I know I'm not. I have reserves within me that flow free at times like this. My instinct to survive is a powerful force.

His knife begins to zero in on me, but I'm fast enough to see it coming. My Hawk eyes pick it out, and my Dasher powers explode, pressing me sideways as the strike comes. In the same motion, my own blade appears from its sheath, and in a moment of sudden calm, I stretch out and send it right into the depths of his body.

Cutting through his armour and abdomen, I feel the razor-sharp blade go deep. Before I pull it out, I give it a firm twist, opening the wound and drawing a heavy roar of agony from the man's throat.

I pull away as he slices again, the adrenaline within him enough to counter the pain and keep him strong for a time. That time, I know, will soon run short. I only need to avoid his strikes until he starts to weaken.

So that's what I do, ducking and diving and moving away as he bears down on me. He sets a trail of red blood as he goes, his side gushing crimson, his scarred face growing quickly pale.

I have no firm knowledge of anatomy yet. I'm not a warrior who can pinpoint an exact area on the human body, knowing that a bullet or blade there will always be fatal. I'm sure my brother is different. I'm sure he can direct his strikes with great precision, fully aware that a direct hit will call an end to that particular foe's time on this earth.

No, that's not me. Not yet. But the stab to this large man's side seemed to be a good one. It looks as though I got lucky, cutting right into some vital organ, his body weakening fast and his attacks growing slow. By the time Zander has dealt with his own opponent, and comes rushing over to help me, he sees that I have already got the job done.

My man is alive, just. His swings are weak and he looks set to fall to his knees. I put him out of his misery with a gunshot to the head, drawing my pistol and sending a bullet to his brain, execution style.

And killing the man, I feel nothing.

Standing together, our two foes defeated, we now turn our eyes down the street. The Stalkers, numbering three, have seemingly faced down with the other five soldiers of the Cure. They clearly sent their greater force there, thinking them the harder task and, most likely, desperate to get through to Cromwell.

And as we look, I feel a slight lurch in my stomach as I see that two more Stalkers are now on the floor. And yet, three still remain fighting.

The realisation comes quick. The two Stalkers defending Cromwell have been forced to join the fight. Now, our grandfather stands alone, vulnerable. And Zander, as he always does, seems to realise just that as quickly as I do.

"Cromwell…" is all he says, before flowing forward towards the fight.

I go straight after him, and see that four of the Cure are still alive, fighting with the three Stalkers. And then I sense more. More of them coming. From the alley, another unit, sneaking through our defences and drawn here to the skirmish.

I grab Zander's arm again and stop him. We turn to the alley and see shapes spreading from the gloom. In a moment of understanding, we look at each and know what needs to be done.

We have to retreat. We cannot hold back this tide.

Rushing towards the fight, we veer left and gallop

straight into the building as the Stalkers continue to engage, providing the distraction we need. We move down a short, crumbling corridor, the building badly damaged, and begin to call out.

"Director Cromwell! Director Cromwell, where are you?"

We stop and listen, but it's so hard to hear much above the battle outside. We call once again, our voices echoing quietly down the silent, grubby corridors and into the apartments that once called home to the denizens of these streets.

Again, no reply comes. Zander points left down a passageway, and then rushes off to the right. He doesn't need to tell me what we need to do.

I gallop away, feeling a slight sense of déjà vu as I go. Not so long ago, my brother and I were doing the same thing in the bowels of the REEF, searching out Adryan before he could be taken for extermination. Now, it isn't for the man I so adore that we're risking our lives, but the very man who put him there.

I call out again as I go, turning my eyes left and right to check the doors. Some are open, others are not. I kick through the latter and scan with my Hawk eyes, thankful that these apartments are small and basic and take little time to check.

I cover the ground quickly, before finally my grandfather comes into view. I don't find him cowering in the corner of some room, praying for his Stalkers to return and take him to safety. In fact, I don't find him at all.

He finds me.

CHAPTER TWENTY FIVE

Returning from one of the apartments, I turn my eyes down the corridor and see my grandfather standing there, his resplendent white suit now growing a shade darker, his hair similarly coloured and pale eyes showing no fear. He looks at me placidly, only a minor crinkle of concern shaping across his brows.

"Cromwell," I stutter, quite surprised to see him before me. "We need to get you out…" I turn and call back down the corridor to my brother. "Zander, I've found him!"

I look back at my grandfather, who steps forward.

"Surprising to see you here, Brie," he says rather calmly. "You two twins really do get around."

"Yeah…sure," I say, anxiously awaiting my brother. "We need to get out of here right away."

"Yes, indeed we do. I fear the battle is going ill."

I should damn well say.

I feel a whoosh of air behind me and turn to find Zander coming into view. He breathes a sigh of relief as he looks upon the Director.

"Director Cromwell, thank God. Come on, this

way, follow me."

We move straight back down to the central corridor, unable now to use our Dasher powers with the old man in tow. To the left, the battle continues outside the building, the Stalkers now sure to be quickly overwhelmed. Going that way would be folly. Cromwell would have no chance at all.

So we go right instead, pressing on towards the rear of the building. Reaching a dead end, Zander pumps up his pulse rifle and asks us to step to the side, before releasing a powerful energy blast that rips straight through the wall. The dust and soot spreads forth, and we press through the gap to find ourselves in an alleyway at the back of the building.

My brother stops for a moment, getting his exact bearings, listening closely to ensure we don't step down the wrong path and into another trap.

"Where now?" I question harshly. "Our plan, Zander…now what?"

It seems to me we've been scuppered, forced to babysit the old man.

"We have to get him to Inner Haven immediately," says my brother, confirming my fears. "This way."

"Hang on," I call. "What about the mission?!"

"Things have changed, Brie. We have a new priority."

A new priority? The thought makes me sick to my bones.

With no time to argue, however, we begin darting eastwards, moving down the alley towards Inner Haven. It's a fair way off, and with Cromwell along for the ride, the going is likely to be slow.

We reach the end and stop, checking left and right. The coast appears to be clear. We head straight for the next street, rushing quickly, Zander calling for us to look for spare vehicles as we go.

I stay back next to my grandfather as Zander leads us on. He moves briskly for an old man, his fairly tall frame covering the ground at a decent clip. Yet, his attire has us sticking out like a sore thumb, and even amid the smog, his white suit is easy to spot.

The voices come from the distance. It seems that we're being tracked again, the Stalkers tasked with protecting Cromwell no longer able to hold back the storm. I imagine they must be dead, overwhelmed as the new soldiers joined in, working through the streets in their small units that seem capable of slipping through our security cordons.

It makes me wonder whether our defence is weakening closer to the perimeter. Have our main blockades over in the west been breached? Are the enemy soldiers here set to have a free run towards Inner Haven now?

Time is running short, and we need to get on with our mission. Colonel Hatcher will no doubt be heading north through the tunnels now, set to hunt down the enemy beyond the wall and disable the men and machines that are their trump cards. If we don't do the same, then it'll be of no use. There's something far more important than the safety of our grandfather at play here…

The shouting in the distance grows louder, and my brother and I turn to see shapes beginning to gather nearby. The hunt is very much on, and we're sure to be quickly run down at this glacial speed.

We reach another street, and head for the shadow of a building, moving into the tenement block and out of sight as the enemy bear down on us. I look at my brother, fixing his gaze firmly.

"Zander, they'll catch us in no time up here," I whisper harshly. "We have to get to the underlands."

"We need a car," he counters. "I…I should go look. You stay here. Stay hidden, stay quiet."

He begins to set off, but I hold him back.

"There's no way I'm letting you go off alone. We'll be surrounded in no time. You'll return to find us both dead."

The mention of my possible death is enough to get him nodding.

"OK. We go on. Follow me, quiet as possible. Director Cromwell, stay low."

We move back out, creeping more slowly now. Through the mist, soldiers seem to be searching, sniffing us out, hunting us down. Only Zander's supreme knowledge of the streets allows us to work through them, working out of the building and through the network of alleys that take us further east.

But it seems inevitable that they'll track us. Our movements begin to grow stifled as we sense more soldiers nearby. We hear their voices, discussing our whereabouts. There are too many. They are too close. We'll never get through alive.

Keeping silent as a spectre, we continue on when we get a chance. But it seems that such silence isn't enough. Here, with the streets a little quieter and further from the perimeter and the battles that rage there, a simple noise, out of turn, could be picked up by a passing Bat.

They have such men with them. Bats to listen for us. Sniffers to smell for us. Hawks to see us through the shroud. Moving faster, it seems we're not accounting for Cromwell's regular, unenhanced eyesight. We may be able to see better through this mist. We may be able to catch sight of obstacles with greater speed and efficiency as we stalk through the shadows. But Cromwell cannot.

And so it's his leg that clatters into a piece of errant debris on the ground. His foot that catches and sends his body falling to the side, and banging into the open door of an abandoned, burnt out car. The door swings shut, his weight pushing it inwards, and clangs loudly into the dark night.

We stop as the sound echoes away through the streets. For a second, nothing seems to happen. And then, sweeping from the distance, voices lift, and boots slam, and soldiers come running.

"Damn it!" grunts Zander. "Move!"

He rushes to Cromwell's side, and I move to his

other. Together, either side of our grandfather, we lurch forward, pressing on with our speed and hauling the old man through the streets. Passing down a narrow path and exiting into a wider road, I spot one of the many shelters here that give protection against the toxic rain.

"Zander," I shout, sending my eyes towards it.

He sees it too, and needs no convincing. We rush right for it, kicking the door open and moving down the stairs into the blackness below. I stop and stand by Cromwell, his face turning queasy from the sudden motion, as Zander quickly moves for the secret passage that gives access to the world below.

It seems we got lucky. Many of these shelters hold such doors, but many do not. And some that do have found themselves blocked and caved in by the recent fighting between our now-friendly forces, impassable and leading to nothing but dead-ends.

But not this one.

As the brick wall opens inward, Zander steps back and grabs hold of Cromwell, dragging him unceremoniously into the tunnel. I follow straight behind as our pursuers reach the top of the stairs outside the shelter, not knowing the city as we do and unsure of just where we've gone.

It gives us precious moments that are the difference between life and death. Pushing the door to the tunnel shut, we escape into the darkness just in time as the soldiers reach the opening. I can hear them banging away wildly as we move away, their weapons chattering and trying to break through.

They will. Soon enough, they'll be right on our tails again. I've escaped through these tunnels before, in very similar fashion to this, and know just how these things work. In no time at all, we'll be under the hammer. We have bought time, but minutes only. It needs to be enough.

As we drag Cromwell through the blackness, knowing full well he cannot possibly see down here, I shout out to my brother, asking where we're going.

The shelter we entered, I know, was in district 5. Not the one we were headed for in district 6, but not too far away. I feel we have no choice now but to continue on. It seems our path is inevitable, as if written by the fates.

"This road leads to the main caverns," calls Zander in reply.

"The waterfall?" I query.

"Yes," he answers.

Our chat is cut short by the sound of pursuit. Echoing through the darkness, the pounding of boots on rock begins to flow our way, following behind a cracking explosion that makes it clear the door has been blasted apart.

The passage is narrow, too narrow to move at great speed in its early expanses. But soon it opens out, allowing us to move either side of our grandfather once again, pressing forward at a speed that will no doubt be extremely uncomfortable and nauseating for the old man.

Were our lives not in such peril, I'd enjoy putting

him through it. But right here, right now, such trivialities are cast aside.

The passage soon opens out and begins to widen, and beyond, the familiar sound of rushing water begins to reach my ears. And the smells of vegetation, too, wafts up my nose, the air growing less close and stuffy, and scented with natural aromas that I once found so pleasant after enduring the rather less agreeable odours of the city above.

The main cavern is close now, vast and wide and spreading through the underlands, a secret garden down in the darkness that once gave me some respite from the dangers above. This passage is one I've never travelled, one of many that enters into the larger cave, ending in a slight drop that requires us to aid Cromwell in reaching the ground.

Zander drops first, hitting the uneven rock floor a couple of metres below, and I'm forced to hold Cromwell tight as I help lower his frame into my brother's arms. It's a level of physical contact I never expected or wished to endure with the man. Unless I've got my hands around his throat, that is...

I drop straight down right after, and we begin working our way into the grand space. The sounds behind us continue to grow, the enemy moving close, and Zander spreads his gaze around the cavern, considering our way out.

There are many routes that lead to dead-ends, and many others that are recently caved in and now obstructed. Zander's knowledge of the place is encyclopaedic, yet he appears frayed and confused, the recent alterations to the structure down here scrambling his memory map.

His eyebrows lower and his movements grow nervous. The rushing of boots in the distance only serves to heighten his panic.

"There's one guaranteed way out," I say. He looks at me with doubt in his eyes. "Zander, we don't have a choice. Maybe we've come here for a reason…"

He doesn't believe such rubbish, and neither do I. This is nothing but a perfect storm, a coincidence. We've been forced right to where we were originally trying to get. Now, we only have one sure choice, and the only difference is that we have Cromwell for baggage.

Very heavy baggage…

"Zander!" I say again. "We have to go, now!"

The movement of the enemy grows ever louder. In mere moments they'll be sure to emerge from the tunnel and hunt us down. Split seconds count, and Zander's doubt isn't helping.

It's time I took charge.

So grabbing my grandfather, who continues to seem disoriented by the entire affair, I gallop forward with all my speed, taking the old man with me. Past rocks piles and pillars I go, surging around the side as I seek the source of the rushing water.

I see it, right ahead, the waterfall tumbling from the rock wall and entering into the pool of ice-cold water. It froths and seethes like a wild beast, ready to gobble up anyone foolish enough to enter its jaws.

I've done so before, and I need to do so again.

It's time to take a dip.

I hear Zander babbling away behind me, but ignore him. I dash for the waterfall and quickly reach the edge, looking down into the pool and the river that flows away into the blackness beneath us. As soon as I step in, that current will take me where I need to go. It will take all of us to safety.

Or kill us in the attempt.

As my brother hurtles up alongside us, I consider leaving Cromwell here to his fate. He'll die for sure, and who knows whether that will activate his remaining Stalkers and Con-Cops to fight against us. How would they even be aware of his demise?

Yet, I can't do it. I can't take the risk. If I leave him here, he'll die for sure. And, well, jumping in the river, he could well drown anyway.

Either way, his fate is no longer fully in our hands. In fact, none of ours are.

With the soldiers now pouring into the cavern a little way away, we have no choice but to enter the maelstrom. And we have to do so now, before they see us, before they can consider following our lead.

So looking at Zander, I take a long breath, urging him to do the same. He has no love for water, and this is going to be some baptism of fire.

"Stay together. Stay afloat," I say.

He nods, and I smile at him nervously.

And with our grandfather still between us, we drop into the raging foam.

CHAPTER TWENTY SIX

The attack of the freezing liquid is enough to set my heart to stone. My insides feel like they're locked in place, and my limbs feel like they're being stabbed all at once by a series of prodding knives.

I hear nothing but a bubbling rush as my head goes under, and make sure to cling tight to Cromwell as we bob for a second as a three, before being sucked right down into the submerged tunnels.

I try to recall the various bends of the river, the various points where the water slows and we can reach the surface and draw breath, but find my memory abandoning me. I have no capacity to think clearly now, all my energy given over to the fight for survival that we all face.

We quickly get sucked through the first underwater portion, before being pressed back to the surface as the world roars again. Zander and I gasp for air, and I open my eyes to draw in what light I can. I see Cromwell's head still under, and reach out to lift him higher. His old face appears, withered and run-down, though he remains conscious and alert enough to heave a mighty gulp of air into his lungs.

The river offers no respite. Sucked under again, we continue to flow further from the waterfall, further from the cavern. Above, the roof of the drowned passages, and the sides of the rock, claw at us with sharp edges. I feel my body dragged to the side, and desperately try to cling onto Cromwell as I go. He's torn from my grasp and my side cracks against the wall, ripping at my combat gear and trying to tear at the skin and flesh beneath.

In the darkness, I open my eyes and find my Hawk powers limited by the white flow of water. I see two shapes ahead, still locked together, and kick hard to rejoin them. I reach them and grip at my grandfather again, and we enter into another cavern and kick together for the surface.

Once again, we break through and gasp, lungs burning and demanding to be refilled. My brother and I work in unison, kicking at the same time, keeping the old man between us. The initial surge gives way to a flatter calm for a moment, drawing us along in the murk, and I note the fear in Zander's eyes, the desperation. I imagine mine must look the same.

The river takes us on, dragging us south beneath the city, taking us closer and closer to the wall and beyond. My limbs grow quickly stiff in the cold, and I think again of just how far the river goes, just how long we'll have to endure this nightmare.

Then my memory wakes, and I remember the passage out. In the depths of the southern quarter, there's a ledge that leads to a tunnel, and that tunnel leads back to the surface. It will, I know, be close to the fighting. It might just lead us into the heart of the enemy as they swarm through the southern breach and take control of the outer portion of the city.

My mind is split in two as we're battered along, crashing into walls and having our clothing ripped and scraped. If we could kick for the ledge together, we could escape this torture and get back to the streets. We could try to find a car, head straight for Inner Haven and get to safety…

But no…no we can't do that.

We have to get outside the city. It's no good going back now. If we reach the ledge and get to the surface, we could very well exit into enemy held territory. We could all be killed right then and there. That won't do at all. We have a job that needs doing, and however much of a gamble it might be, we have to try.

I battle with the two options as we go, until suddenly we reach the cave where the ledge awaits. I'm on the left, nearest to it. As we break the surface of the water, I hear Zander's wild voice calling for us to make for land.

"Kick, Brie," he splutters. "Kick!"

I look at the ledge, and recall how close I was to making it when I was down here last. I got a grip of the rock, but was dragged away by the furious current. I had no idea where the river would take me from there. I thought, at that moment, that I would die.

But this time, I know the ledge isn't where we need to go. I have to trust my instincts. I have to take charge. I won't let us abandon this mission for the sake of our grandfather. His life may very well be important. But there's something bigger at stake here.

So as my brother calls desperately for me to kick and reach for the rock, I don't. I kick the other way instead, doing so in secret so he doesn't know, working with the current to keep us away from the water's edge. His legs, powerful, churning through the froth, aren't enough to get us all there alone. I deny him, and bit by bit, the water takes us away.

As my brother exclaims and roars out, depleting his stocks of energy, I shout for him to stop.

"It's a lost…cause," I call into the echoing, rushing chamber, spitting water that surges into my mouth. "The wat…waterfall…it's close…"

I kick a few more times, and turn my back from the ledge as if to show I'm done trying to get there.

"Save your…energy," I say. "Stop kicking."

It's only Zander's efforts that are now keeping us from being swallowed back up. But slowly, he realises they're futile. And as he stops the fight, we're quickly drawn further downriver, my grandfather still staying quiet between us, just trying to breathe when he can, his old limbs unable to provide much horsepower as we drive our way onwards.

We're close now, and I know it. At this point in

my last venture here, I was all set to give up. I had no idea where I was being taken. I had no idea when the torment would end. Only when I reached the waterfall, well beyond the southern gate, and was spat out into the pool below, did I realise I'd made it.

Then, of course, I had plenty more battles to come.

This time is different. We need to get to where we're going. We need to reach that pool and survive the thirty-metre drop. We need to quickly gather our senses and continue the fight. And we need to do it all while keeping our grandfather alive.

So on we go, battered and bruised, freezing and exhausted, tumbling beneath the surface before being thrust again to the top. For another few minutes, we suffer the ride, and I call out when I can that the opening is coming, that the end is near.

Then the light appears, though not as it was before. Last time, it was night, but the moonlight was bright, the end of the tunnel so obvious in the darkness. This time, the smog holds that light at bay, and above, the sky is filled with natural clouds too, the world hidden under several heavy blankets.

But, still, my Hawk eyes are enough to see the end. And the growing roar of the waterfall is another piece of evidence that our journey is about to conclude.

"Deep breath!" I shout. "Brace for the fall. It's a long drop!"

I hold onto my grandfather even tighter than ever

as the water and passage straighten out, and turn to see the grit in my brother's eyes. He stares forward, ready for what's set to come his way, the roar growing ever louder.

Then, with the water speeding towards its end, I see the faint signs of the forest beyond, now so different to before. It's been eaten away, the fires still raging far off to the south as the inferno continues to spread to the distance. But immediately ahead, the woods are black, the world burnt, lit only with the embers of the dying flames.

It gives some shape to the world ahead as we reach the river's end and the waterfall's beginning. As I call once more for us to brace, I feel the world give way beneath us for a split second as we're tossed out into the void. Down below, the black pool of water awaits, rushing up so fast I barely have time to shut my eyes and clench my jaw as the surface slaps us hard.

We crash and tumble, and this time I cannot hold on. I'm ripped from the others, the three of us split apart, churning in the froth for a few long seconds before I burst for the surface. I crash through, gulping air, and see my brother do the same.

But not Cromwell. He's nowhere to be seen.

I share a look with my twin. Our eyes regain their power, darting left and right and scanning fast. He must be beneath the water. Without a second's hesitation, we dive and search, kicking hard and moving quickly for the bottom.

Neither of us truly know how to swim, yet our

instincts give us the necessary ability to do so. And our Dasher powers rise to the fore once more, the kicks of our legs and the clawing of our hands sufficiently speedy and powerful to have us rushing through the water like hunting fish.

Floating at the bottom, I see a shape in the darkness. I thrash for it and the form of Cromwell appears, eyes closed, body limp. I grab him, press my feet to the muddy floor, and leap with all I have, forcing us both to the silver surface.

We smash through the veil, and Zander quickly swims over, the two of us awkwardly paddling for shore and taking Cromwell with us. We reach the muddy bank, and heave him onto the sopping earth, his white suit sodden and covered in filth, his eyes still shut and body still.

Zander quickly leans in, setting his ear to Cromwell's mouth.

"He's not breathing," he says. "I need to resuscitate him. He cannot die!"

I watch, exhausted, as I sit in the mud, wondering how it's come to this. Wondering how I've just been forced to save the man who killed my parents, who led to the deaths of so many others. Wondering how, right now, Zander is having to bring him back to life, when he lies there, seemingly dead.

A large part of me watches and hopes my brother fails as he pumps at his chest, and sets his lips to the old man's, breathing into his mouth and doing the work of his dormant lungs. I wish to stop him, hold him back, let Cromwell cling to death and not let go.

It's his. He deserves it. Let him keep it.

But I don't interfere, because there's another part that needs him to live. A part that cannot be sure if his death will be our undoing. If he dies, right now, maybe everyone I love will follow. Maybe the entire city will be consumed in the hours to come.

So I watch, torn, shivering and sodden and entirely afraid of both outcomes. My brother pumps and breathes, growing ever more frantic and desperate. He isn't torn like me. He doesn't know what I know. He desires only for the old man to spit that water from his lungs and return to the world of the living.

And as all hope seems to fade, and the already pale skin of Cromwell appears to lose all remaining colour, I lean back and accept that my grandfather is no more. I can barely think of the victory of it all, of the joy this moment should bring. It's something I want so dearly, more than anything in the world. To see it rid of the man who took away my family. The man who has caused so much suffering and grief.

But there is no joy there for me. There's just an emptiness as I watch him continue to fade, Zander's efforts now fading too. I reach over, and lay my hand on my brother's back, and say softly, "It's over. You did all you could…"

He leans back, eyes narrow, teeth tightly clenched together. And for a second, all goes quiet and still, and I barely even think of the wailing machine nearby, and the chattering gunfire much further away.

We sit there, locked in time, next to the body of

Director Cromwell. And what must only be a second or two seems to last an age.

With my hand still on Zander's back, I feel him move away again. It's sudden, his hands reaching out one final time, pressing at Cromwell's chest in a final surge, breathing through his lips with a final blow.

I consider the effort wasted. But what do I know?

As if by some awful miracle, Artemis Cromwell stirs. His body and neck seem to convulse, and his mouth opens wide as a gush of dirty water comes pouring out. Zander leans back in surprise, and Cromwell's lungs pull in a breath sharp enough to cut steel.

His eyes open, pale and cold, and a trickle of colour returns to his sallow cheeks. He looks to Zander above him, and I see a brand new emotion in his eyes. I see something he's never displayed.

I see thanks. A deep and very real gratitude.

His lips open, quivering a touch, as if such an experience is enough to cause a break in even the most cold and callous of minds. They try to speak, his stare refusing to leave Zander's face, a few inaudible croaks breaking from his throat.

"It's OK, Director Cromwell," says Zander, smiling and panting hard. "You're going to be just fine."

Yes. Unfortunately, he is.

CHAPTER TWENTY SEVEN

Director Cromwell's state of consciousness appears to be a false dawn. As he lies there in the mud, staring at my brother, his eyes fade off again, flickering before falling shut.

Zander's quick to do his checks once more, ensuring the old man is breathing and has just passed out. He has. Again, I'm in two minds about that.

Only once my brother's confirmed that Cromwell is still alive does he now fall back onto the bank, breathing heavily and expelling all the tension from his body. He shakes his head in relief and croaks, "That was far too close for comfort."

I allow him a few moments in the mud to regain his energy as I stand and perform a quick check of our surroundings. It's still smoky here, yet not like in the city. The smoke is thinner, billowing about on the breeze and being coughed up from fires still burning not too far away. It appears, too, to be flowing somewhat in the direction of the city, as if drawn there by some invisible force.

And all I can think is that he's out there. Someone, some wind manipulator, is out there keeping the city shrouded and hidden. Maintaining the veil for his soldiers to use for cover.

Over the rushing waterfall, the sound of wailing is also close. A little through the burning woods, away off to the east along the ridge. That's where the horrible noise is coming from, closer now than ever, drawing us in. We cannot delay too long. We have to take it out.

I move back to my brother and find him sitting up. He's checking his pulse rifle to ensure it's still operational. I do the same and find mine in good working order. We check our other firearms too. They all appear to be just fine, undamaged by the water and violent journey down the river.

Finally, Zander draws the radio from the pouch in his belt. The pouch appears to be waterproof, though I think I see a rip in it. He begins fiddling with the settings, trying to get in touch with Colonel Hatcher away on the other side of the outerlands beyond the city. It's no use. The radio fizzes and spits sparks, dripping water.

"Damn," growls Zander, tossing the radio to the mud. "It's broken." He sucks in a breath and shakes his head, standing to his feet. "It's OK," he says, as if trying to reassure himself, and me. "It's fine. Hatcher will get the job done. We need to focus on ours."

"And what about *him*?" I ask, glaring at Cromwell.

Zander looks around. As far as I see it, we have to leave Cromwell here. There's no way he's coming with us.

"How about there," I say, pointing towards a collection of rocks near the cliff. "We put him there, do the job, and then come fetch him after…"

Zander looks to be having a more difficult time than me making this decision. He's anything but indecisive, but right now that unwanted trait appears to be creeping into his character.

Usually, it would be him quickly making decisions. But, in this case, I'm of a very clear mind about what we need to do.

"Look, Zander, we don't have time to consider this," I say. "We can't take Cromwell with us, right?"

He shakes his head.

"No…"

"Good," I go on. "And we're here now, so there's no getting him back to the city yet. Priority one is disabling that machine and seeing what else is out there. The Director will have to wait."

He starts nodding.

"OK, you're right. Let's get him over by the rocks. Help me out."

Together, we lift Cromwell to his feet, dripping water and mud and looking quite unlike his old self, and drag him over to the cliffs. During my first time here, I was quite aware that the toxic fog wasn't an issue around the water's edge, only collecting by the trees and not on the shore. It seems, right now, that it isn't an issue at all.

By the looks of things, the fire that consumed the woods has eaten the poisonous fumes as well. Perhaps that was yet another benefit for the Cure in setting the forest aflame. Now, replacing the toxic smog is a smog of smoke instead. It's quite unpleasant, but seemingly far less potent and dangerous than what came before. And hidden here, Artemis Cromwell should be perfectly safe.

Reaching the rocks, we haul him through a narrow gap and into a small cave-like formation. It has a low ceiling and tight walls, the space hardly big enough to accommodate the three of us as we tuck the old man in.

"Right, we need to tie him up," I say as we lay him onto the cold stone.

Zander frowns at me.

"Tie him? Why?"

"*Because*," I say, as if the word is explanation enough.

"Because….what?"

"Are you being deliberately obtuse, brother? We need to make sure he stays where he is."

"He will. Why on earth would he leave this place alone and try to get back to the city? He'd die a dozen times before he got there. He's not a stupid man, Brie, however much you seem to think he is."

"And what does that mean?" I query.

"Just what I said," he tells me. "You have a hate for Director Cromwell that seems to go well beyond all others. You still let your emotions direct you more than you should…"

I feel my blood boiling, my nerves frayed. I shake my head and mutter, "Yeah, but you don't know what I know."

I immediately regret the words, and my following expression and mannerisms probably make it clear I'm hiding something.

"Enlighten me. What do you know, Brie?"

He peers into me through the darkness in that small, claustrophobic cave. I turn my gaze from him, refusing to connect, hiding my thoughts. Yet my feelings are enough for him gauge regardless. My guilt, my shame. It's all there for him to sense and feel. He knows that I'm not telling him something.

"Look, we need to get going," I huff, moving for the opening.

He steps in my way.

"No, not yet," he says.

"Zander! What the hell are you doing? We're in a fight for our lives here. We don't have time for this."

"Make time," he growls. "Tell me what you know."

His words are intense, his eyes equally so. I stand ahead of him, still peering everywhere but into his keen eyes. That in itself is a clear sign of guilt.

"Zander," I say again, more calmly this time,

drawing a breath. "I just think that it's best to tie Cromwell up, that's all. I don't think it's sensible to leave him here alone without taking precautions…"

"Stop," he says flatly. "Don't change the subject."

"But this *is* the subject! The only one that matters right now…"

"No, there's something more going on." He stops a moment, and then says, "It's…it's about our mother, isn't it?"

I flash my eyes to his and smile awkwardly. I have no idea how to behave in such situations. My ability to hold the truth, to lie, when thoughts of my mother are swirling through my mind, is non-existent. I'm not skilled at this at all. My emotions, that I apparently can't control, are starting to get the better of me.

"Our mother? What…what are you talking about?" I stammer.

"I heard you, Brie," he says. "I heard you talking with West in the Fangs' village a few days ago. He said our father's name, Maxwell. And…our mother's too. He called her Elisa."

He draws his hand forward and raises my chin, lifting it. I continue to keep my eyes elsewhere.

"You know her name," he says softly. "How do you know her name?"

I recoil from him, pressing back towards the rock and shaking my head. Thoughts of her past and our father's past flow through my head. Here, in this small cave, with the culprit unconscious at our feet,

265

and the war raging outside, I only have thoughts for them.

"I don't…you must have misheard…"

My eyes glance down at Cromwell, a ripple of anger working across my face. My brother moves forward a pace. He sees. He sees everything.

"The truth, it must be hard for you to tell," says Zander, his voice flattening out. "It's him, isn't it?" He looks to our grandfather. "This is about him."

I look at the old man too, and then turn my eyes up to my brother's. He's suddenly calm and relaxed, not trying to force the truth from me, not compelling me to speak. He deserves to know. He's always deserved to know.

And I can't keep it from him any longer.

I'm sorry, grandmother. I'm sorry…

I begin to nod, my heart-rate starting to flare.

"It's about him," I confirm.

My words seem to be all Zander needs. The pieces begin to gather and form into a clear picture in his head. I look right into his eyes, and see the calm frown lower, and see behind them into his mind as the truth begins to settle. He looks at Cromwell, and then up at me. He takes a breath and speaks.

"Say it," he whispers.

He knows. He knows now.

"He's….he's our grandfather," I say, still reluctant.

Zander draws a breath, quite sharp. He shuts his eyes for a long moment. When he opens them, he stares right at me.

"And Lady Orlando," he whispers. "She's our grandmother."

"Yes," I say weakly. "She...she wanted to tell you."

He lifts his hand and gestures for me to go silent. I do so immediately. His head starts shaking.

"If she wanted to tell me, she would have done," he says plainly, calmly.

He looks again at Cromwell, staring at the old man's face. I know just how hard this is. I've experienced it before. But, for him it must be harder discovering the truth. He's lived this life for so much longer than me.

Yet, he's taking it well. He isn't like me with his emotions. He will be working through it in his mind, letting the truth sink in. I wonder - has he suspected it for a while?

So I ask, tentatively, and he withdraws from his brief reverie and looks at me again.

"I thought...something. I believed Lady Orlando was hiding something. She never let me look in her head. She knew there were things I couldn't see."

"*Couldn't* see? You understand why she hid the truth?"

He nods slowly, so mature in taking the news.

"I trust her," he tells me. "I always have. I trust

her to make the right decisions, to do what's best for me. She's…she's my grandmother," he says, a smile beginning to burgeon.

Then he drops his eyes and sees Cromwell again, and the smile disappears, replaced by a frown.

"And he's my grandfather," he whispers, voice dull and low.

I leave him to his thoughts again for a few moments, until another question rises on his lips. A question I don't want to field right now.

"How did you find out?" he asks me. "Elisa…our mother. She was their daughter? Daughter of Director Cromwell, of Lady Orlando…"

He's speaking as though to himself, as if he needs to vocalise it now to believe it. To fully believe it.

"I…found his files in the archives," I say. "I was looking for information on our father, Maxwell. I found Director Cromwell's file instead."

"And that revealed his next of kin?" he asks.

I nod.

He considers it once more, taking a moment to himself. I can see the many queries bubbling up inside his head, this conversation one not to be had now. We have work to do, people relying on us. We need to get moving.

But I have to be careful now. I can't rush him. I need his mind to be clear and on point for the fight ahead.

"We should think about getting moving, Zander,"

I whisper gently but with a note of urgency. "We don't have much time."

Once more, he pulls away from his daydream, from his internal considerations. He steps a little closer to me, and takes hold of my cheeks.

"I need to see," he says. "I need to know it all."

I work up a reply but don't express it. Time is too short for words, and my mind holds all the answers that he can quickly find for himself.

So I don't speak, but merely open my eyes wide, and take a breath as he sets his gaze to them. He darts inside, and I feel him immediately searching for all my knowledge of our parents, of what happened to them. And as he does, I see the memories flooding back, the recent reveals, the truths told by Lady Orlando, happening right before my eyes once more.

It happens so quickly. There's so little to really see. So little that I actually know. But I know enough. I know that it was Artemis Cromwell, our grandfather, who ordered the executions of our parents, and of our grandmother. I know that only the latter escaped, freed by a final act of bravery by our mother. I know that our parents will have suffered terribly, if not physically, but mentally, knowing that they'd never be able to see us grow, become the people we are today.

I know it all. And now, so does Zander.

And pulling away, I see the cracks appearing in his façade. I see the same hate that I hold for our grandfather starting to brew. I see a shimmering vein of anger set in his bloodshot eyes.

He turns, one final time, to look at Cromwell. And drawing a sudden, fierce breath, he looks set to strike.

I reach out quickly, seeing it coming, seeing him about to lose his cool, and take hold of him. I wrap my arm over him in a manner to both restrain and calm. And I whisper softly, cooling his burning ire.

"Don't, Zander," I say. "Don't do it. You're stronger than that."

I find my own words slightly ironic. Only minutes ago, I was wishing Cromwell dead, and Zander was trying his very best to keep him alive. Now, it appears my duty to hold back the storm myself, to save my grandfather's life as I already have this night.

As we both have.

His madness quickly settles, suppressed beneath the surface. He turns away from Cromwell with a snarl and shakes his head.

"*I* saved his life. *You* saved his life. And he…he killed our parents."

"I know, I know," I say soothingly. "We'll get our revenge, brother. We'll get it together. But not now. Not yet. We have something more important to do."

I look right into his hazel eyes and show him we're in this together. All the way, the two of us against the world. We'll save the city. We'll make Cromwell pay. We will. We have to.

He fills his lungs once more and I see the change in his eyes. Then he guides them down to our grandfather, still unconscious on the floor.

"You're right, Brie," he snarls. "Let's tie him up. Nice and tight."

He drops a wink for my benefit, and I smile. And together, we bind the old man so he cannot move in inch.

CHAPTER TWENTY EIGHT

"Are you sure you have your thoughts straight, brother? You need to focus now."

Zander smiles at me as we move from the cave and little network of rocks near the cliff. The rushing of the waterfall grows louder, as does the wailing not too far away. And through the smoke, the burnt out woods become clear.

He nods, loosening up.

"I'm fine, Brie, really. I...in a way I'm glad."

"Glad?"

"Glad I know the truth now," he explains. "I told you once before that I didn't think about our parents much. I told you that I'd probably never know the truth, so there was no point in worrying about it. I guess I lied to you. I've never stopped wondering, hoping to know who they really were, what happened to them. It sounds awful, because of what they had to go through...but I'm happy I know. I feel...lighter somehow." He shakes his head and looks away. "That probably makes no sense..."

"No, no, it really does," I say, pulling him into a sudden hug. "It makes perfect sense, Zander. I felt the exact same thing when I found out."

He smiles at me again.

"Well, we are twins, after all."

"Yeah," I laugh, before frowning and realising laughter has no place here. "So you're definitely OK?"

He nods and looks back to the cave.

"We'll deal with him later. Now let's go save the city, what do you say?"

"Sure. Walk in the park, right?"

We share tense looks, hidden by smiles.

"Yeah. Nothin' to it."

From the edge of the small lake, we turn our collective attention over to the east, where the wailing appears to be emanating from. It sounds close, a little louder than it did from the perimeter of the city, suggesting it's a similar distance from the wall as it is from where we are now. By the angles, I'd imagine it's about five hundred metres away, or thereabouts. But then, that's nothing but a guess.

Zander concurs with the estimate, and we begin making our way around the lake and towards the burnt woodlands beyond. Still, many stumps of trees are smouldering, and many pillars of smoke are billowing into the air. The fume is endless, yet thinner here, the fire having passed further south where it still rages strong.

The smoke, however, helps to warm the air. My previous journey down the river had ended with me quivering in the cold, desperately trying to grow warm in the early morning sun. Now, the shiver to my blood has all but left me, the burning world and family drama sufficient to cast away the biting chill.

The same will hopefully be true of Cromwell. Or else we'll return to find our grandfather an icicle. On second thoughts, perhaps that wouldn't be so bad…

We work our way towards the cliff on the eastern side of the lake, our clothes still sodden and caked in mud. We take a few moments to wash ourselves clean before venturing on, the mud only likely to weigh us down in a fight. It might only be minor, but slowing by an inch could be enough to get you killed out here. Best to take no chances.

More worrying is the fact that the journey down the river must have drained our energy quite significantly. I certainly feel it, now that the adrenaline is seeping away, and can only imagine that Zander's stocks are being quickly depleted. He hasn't slept for quite some time, and the exertions in the cold water will only have served to make matters worse.

As we prepare to enter the fuming woods, I take a moment to ensure he's ready. It's a rare turnaround for me to be asking such a thing of him. Usually, it's the other way around.

"I'm fine, Brie," he assures me. "I can go on for nights without rest if I have to."

I have to take his word for it, yet the evidence suggests otherwise. I've found Zander to be quite grouchy on certain mornings when he's had little rest. The cumulative effect of several nights without sleep would surely make him unbearable, and the resulting impact on his ability to fight would be severe.

Still, we have no choice. We cannot stop and rest, not even for a moment. Every second we delay, more lives will be lost. That thought alone is plenty to refuel our tanks.

So we move straight on, clothing cleaned of mud and grit and given a fresh coating of cool water. The woods right ahead, beneath the cliffs, once thick and tangled and replete with the murky green mist, have changed completely. They're now fitted with stumps and glazed in black ash, the cover of the trees something we can hardly rely upon.

The woods here are peppered with marshlands too. The little clearings where the swamps were set between the trees are now nothing but pools of tar, the toxic water turned black. They are easy to see and avoid, and while we have little cover from the thickets, we are largely hidden amid the smoke.

And, mercifully, there are plenty of rock formations here too. These woodlands are quite different from those in which Rhoth and the Fangs dwell, over to the northwest of here. And far different from the forests up in the mountains, where the trees grow tall and are widely dispersed, and the air is thin and clean, an invigorating tonic compared to what lies below.

No, these lands are very different indeed. They are swamps, really, with ugly gatherings of trees in between. A network of bogs and mires and unpleasant glades, with stumps and trunks and burning boles littering the land. The rocks, too, are burnt black, set here and there amid the quagmire, the entire place little more than a nightmare. A vision of the world the Cure exist in, the world they leave behind.

Zander doesn't know these lands quite so well. The Nameless stayed mostly to the north, though often found themselves heading west too. The south was considered a redundant land, a putrid place with little to offer them.

Yet my brother's vast knowledge of the world around the city isn't required, not this time. We are drawn only to the wailing, which grows louder with each step, moving from rock to rock and between what cover remains, always stopping and listening and looking for what lies ahead.

With the noise becoming so deafening, the sounds of the war, raging off in the city, grow silent to our ears. Our ability to communicate verbally is also drowned out, so we turn to our telepathic link to speak if we need to. Moving just ahead of me, leading the way, I hear Zander constantly telling me to stop, get low, be silent, his words clear in my mind, even over the din.

I follow each order with impeccable timing and efficiency, trusting my brother's instincts. Here, in the wilds, we could stumble upon the enemy at any moment. We are quite aware that their army marched from the west, and quite aware too that the majority of their forces will now have entered the city.

But nevertheless, we need to be careful. They will no doubt have soldiers still here beyond the wall, and here in the south where one of their breaches was devised. For all we know, there could still be hundreds of them crawling these lands. And we can be certain that they'll have some soldiers posted at the source of this racket. We just have to hope that their forces here are limited.

As we draw ever closer, the deafening scream becomes almost unbearable. It's so high pitched it seems to cut right into my brain, my eardrums threatening to explode. We stop to consider some combat to the assault, and Zander improvises by ripping off some fabric from his gear and fashioning rudimentary earplugs.

We set them deep and find that it helps, before adding a coating of mud in order to further seal off the hole. The sense of relief is profound, though it will make it much harder to hear for the enemy. Then again, the shrieking is so loud that our capacity to do so is rather mute anyway, and given how we can communicate telepathically, we have some advantage.

With our ears now protected, and the wailing somewhat dulled, we move on once more. The smoke, still pouring from further south, continues to be spread towards the city, more obviously now as we grow near. What breeze there is drifts westwards, suggesting that the smoke should, if following the natural course of things, be heading to the west as well. The fact that it seems to be floating northward from here is indicting. There is someone here doing this. This isn't natural at all.

From the lake, we must have covered several hundred metres. They must be close, and yet we haven't seen a soul so far. The smog, thinner here, presents enough detail for our Hawk eyes to see a decent way ahead. It's only a matter of time before they spot what we're here for.

The ground continues to fluctuate, its shape never constant. We avoid the pools of black poison, and the creatures that dwell within. Yet our worries of the Shadows of the outerlands, and the beasts that lurk in the wilds, are absent at this time. Most will no doubt have abandoned these places, the burning woods scaring them away, destroying the lands they hunt. They will uproot and seek more bountiful pastures, returning perhaps when the wailing is done, and the smoke is gone, and the lands are littered with the dead upon which to feast.

Soon enough, a great buffet may be laid down for them, attracting all beasts from far and wide. But not yet. Now, they hold to the distant shadows, biding their time, ready to scavenge what they can from the wreckage of the world.

We pay them no mind, and focus only on the threat ahead. Working down a slope into a little valley, a cluster of rocks and a clearing beyond finally shows us the light. Through the mist, shapes appear. Not those of tree stumps and rocks, but the unmistakable forms of men, and the straight lines of structures that suggest they've fashioned a camp.

We stop at the rocks, and look each other right in the eye.

That's it, I hear my brother say in my mind. *We've found it.*

He orders for me to stay back as he, very gently now, creeps around to the side of the rocks and sends his gaze beyond. I watch him as he scans through the burnt down trees and smog, his hazel eyes intense as they work up a picture of what we're facing.

As he does so, I hear him speaking to me in my head. He doesn't need to turn back to me to do so. He merely commentates mentally on what he's seeing, updating me in real time via our telepathic link.

A small force, he says. *I see...five soldiers. Perhaps more within the tents. There are two of them. A soldier standing guard outside each one. Three other soldiers watching the flanks. None are looking this way.*

How big are the tents? I ask.

Not large. About a dozen square metres. One a bit bigger than the other. Perhaps holding supplies.

And the machine?

I...I see it, yes. Other side of the camp. Oh...more soldiers there. Three more I think, hard to see in the fog. It's quite large, square shape, metal. It looks...vulnerable. Like a grenade would do the job.

He scans a little more, looking left and right beyond the camp for possible entry points, before withdrawing and returning to me.

Now, making eye contact, we resume our discussion.

We need to work around the other side, he informs me. *Get closer to the sonic machine. It'll be shielding our movements, just like it did theirs. They won't hear us coming, Brie. We'll make their own machine work against them.*

And eights soldiers, you say? I ask.

That's all I saw.

What about the wind-manipulator? Someone's sending this smoke into the city, Zander. We need to destroy them too.

We will, comes his voice in my mind, firm and unbending. *We may learn more on the eastern side of the camp. Follow me. We need to backtrack a bit, then go around.*

We head off again, stepping away and keeping low, before working further to the south and then moving east. The source of the noise, now known, is kept at the right distance, guiding us as we curve around through the marshlands and make for the other side.

The journey takes another ten or so minutes, precious moments that we don't want to waste and yet cannot hurry. In order to be safe, we probably move further from the camp than we need to, yet it's the right call to do so given the stakes.

Working closer again, we find more rocks behind which to hide, this time on the eastern flank of the little base. It is clearly only minor, the vast majority of the Cure's army now within the city. Yet it's big enough of a challenge to make us extremely careful. So far, we've seen eight soldiers, but there are likely to be more. And if we're not careful, and they spot us before we can strike, we'll surely be overrun.

Once again, Zander scans ahead, his eyesight better than mine, and his mind for strategy too. He informs me that the machine is set to the side, largely unprotected. The three soldiers there appear unconcerned by the noise, all of them with protective blockers on their ears. They don't seem to sense a threat. This may just be our chance.

Before we act, however, I find my attention turning north. Just to the front of the camp, I see the dust and smoke moving in an odd way. It seems to swirl in all directions, only just visible now from this closer vantage.

Zander, I say, getting his attention.

He looks upon it too from the side of the rocks, and turns to me with a glint in his eyes.

You were right, Brie, he says. *You were right all along...*

It's him. There's someone there, keeping the city in the shroud. Kill him. Destroy the machine. Wipe out the lot of this vermin.

And maybe, just maybe...turn the battle in our favour.

We quickly form a plan to do just that. We will use our speed, and the cover of the noise and the smoke to make our move. We'll act before they know what's hit them, and disable as many of them as possible with our grenades. We'll disorient them, turning their advantage against them, and will free the city from their grip.

At least, that's the plan…

CHAPTER TWENTY NINE

My role is clearly defined, and pretty darn important.

As Zander slips away from the rocks, moving off to the south and then to the west, I crouch, hidden out of sight, awaiting the instruction to attack.

He disappears almost immediately into the mist, once more moving beyond the sight of our enemy and retracing the route we've just taken. Within minutes, he'll be back on the western side of the camp. It won't take him ten to return. He knows just where he's going now, and will get there as quick as he can.

I brace myself as I prepare to spring, my pulse rifle across my lap, a set of three grenades ready to be launched. In my head, I hear my brother's updates, informing me of where he is. Before I know it, he's telling me he's moving back for the rocks on the western edge at the bottom of the slope, the clearing just beyond and the camp within it.

OK, one more time, I hear him say. *When I say so, slip as close as you can and toss your grenades at the sonic machine. Roll them low, and keep out of sight. I'll do the same here, and just as they go off, we attack. Got it?*

Got it, I say. *When you're ready, brother.*

I draw a long breath and steady my breathing. My heart-rate steadies too, pumping loudly in my ears. I shift to the side of the rocks and shoulder my rifle, gathering up the three grenades.

And then I hear him.

OK. GO! NOW! he says.

I act without hesitation or even minor delay, because I know he won't. Staying as low as possible, I plant one leg in front of the other, moving between stumps of trees and within the thick smoke that hovers close to the ground. The soldiers ahead, all three of them, meander about casually near the sonic machine, which grows in clarity as I get near. I look upon it, but don't understand it. To me, it's just some box emitting the most awful of sounds. I care little for how it was made or what from. All I care about is that it can be destroyed.

Pressing as close as I dare, I begin arming the three grenades, flipping the switch on each. The first, I roll through the mush, making sure there's no pool of toxic water nearby for it to disappear into. It doesn't, but swiftly glides towards the sonic machine, bobbling near as I set the other two on their paths.

One, I roll a little further from the machine, over to the north where the soldiers wander. It works towards their feet, seemingly unnoticed, close enough to tear one to shreds and perhaps maim or even kill the others. I'll find out momentarily.

The final grenade isn't rolled, but thrown with more force. I have to shift a little to toss it far enough, hurling it with all my might high through the air and into the swirling mist ahead where I know the wind-manipulator to be. As it begins its journey, high over the camp and as yet unseen, the first goes off, its fuse complete.

Right ahead, perhaps twenty metres away, I feel the punch of burning air press me backwards. The explosion is violent and sudden, and joined within the blink of an eye by another, not far away on the other side of the camp. Then another, my second grenade, fills the air with yet another boom a split second later, right before the three soldiers can act. And another of Zander's, targeting the tents and soldiers to the western side, follows.

They all pop, one after another, as I tumble into the mire with the force of the detonation. It's more powerful than I thought, the blast radius larger. Boom, boom, boom, they go. For several seconds, our coordinated assault fills the space ahead in fire and black smoke, and then my final grenade rips through the northern edge of the base too.

It takes me a moment to regain my faculties to the point where I realise that the wailing has stopped. As the ringing of the explosions filters from my blocked ears, and the vibrations leave my body, I note that my first grenade did its job well. And my second, by the sight of the blood and errant limbs that scatter the ground ahead, did so too.

Beyond that, I can't tell.

I call out for my brother in my head.

Zander! Are you OK?! What now?

His response is immediate, and frenetic.

Now we fight, sister! We send them all to hell!

His voice is wild and buoyant in my mind, and through the mist I see the blue energy boiling at the tip of his gun across the camp. It builds and builds and then bellows forth, spreading for what remains of the camp ahead. The entire place is now lit in fire, and with the wailing noise gone, I hear a different sort of screaming reach my ears, muffled through my rudimentary plugs.

The source is as clear as that of the sonic machine. Several men rush about, their clothing wreathed in fire, searching for some pool of acid water into which to fall. I see the blue energy of my brother's pulse rifle cut one of them down, and then another, oblivious to his presence, sees his torment quickly ended.

A third, however, isn't so lucky. He's unfortunate enough to stumble upon a bog, and while dropping in puts out the flame, it certainly doesn't offer much relief. Instead of fire, his flesh is quickly burned by the toxic water, so potent in these parts, and he continues to scream and thrash until the pain becomes too much and he passes out, plunging into the mire.

I hear my brother calling again for me to enter, and realise that there are more soldiers to deal with. Those not killed in the blasts or the fire, or cut down by Zander's rifle, quickly realise what's going on, emerging from burning tents and trying to gather their wits.

Swinging my own rifle from my shoulder, I rush up from the earth and spit fire their way. My gun spews in a beautiful shade of blue like Zander's, and from both sides, the camp is assaulted. Trapped in a snare, and disorientated as we hoped they'd be, the soldiers rush wildly and don't work as one. Not knowing just where the threat is coming from until it's too late, they stumble into our net, and pay the most precious price of all.

I begin moving forward, and see that the smoke is beginning to clear. It's enough to be noticeable, and the direction of its travel has changed too. No longer does it resist the wind, moving north rather than west. Now, it flows as it should, the breeze taking it with it as it gently glides off to the west.

All I can think is that we must have got him. The wind-manipulator must be dead.

I'm wrong.

It's a sudden blast of air that proves it. From my right, the rush of wind is as strong as the explosion, pushing me straight back and off my feet. It comes from nowhere, completely out of the blue, bits of grit and mud and dirt coming with it. They spray into my face and eyes and momentarily blind me, and I instinctively call for Zander for help as I hit the floor, winded.

I wipe my face clean and blink away the grime, setting my eyes in the direction of the sudden attack.

The smoke ahead of me seems to have almost cleared entirely, but beyond it grows thick, hiding what lies within. I turn to grab my weapon, discarded to the side, and try to lift it and pepper the shroud with fire.

I don't get the chance. Another press of air comes, all that murk and gathered smoke rushing at me. It's more violent this time, and with it larger bits of debris begin to spray towards me, stones and chunks of rock and wood, even blown off limbs that trail red blood as they advance.

The wind continues to build, and my mind harkens back to when Kira was taken. I was impotent then in the face of a wind-manipulator. Assaulted from all sides and unable to lift my weapon in the storm. Soon, that storm became a tornado that was far too much for us all to bear. I cannot let that happen again. This unnatural weather needs to be quelled right here.

I leave my pulse rifle where it is. It's only weighing me down.

I stay still, lie low, and gather all the strength I have.

I look up, and focus on large bits of debris as they come – trunks and branches and bodies – and dodge any that get too near.

And then, when I'm ready, I make my move.

Through the furious wind, I set first to my knees, then move into a crouch, and then let my legs carry me forward. I utilise all the Dasher power I have, marching forward against the storm as I hear Zander's voice calling for me. He's lost somewhere within it too, off to the side of the camp in his own battles. I can't rely on him here.

I don't want to rely on him either.

The storm is growing fast, and my target remains hidden. But if I can't see him, he surely can't see me. I begin thrashing my legs as much as I can, working against the wind, scrapping forward with all I have until I reach the smog.

It's so strong now that I have to drop back to my knees. I use my hands to rip through the earth, all but crawling on all fours. I scrape and inch my way into the maelstrom, my strength waning, my lungs and legs and arms burning. I could so easily let go, be flung far and wide off into the blackened forest. I could let the torture end right here.

But no. I won't. I'll never give up, never give in.

It's my duty to succeed.

So with a final surge, I creep into the blackness and the swirling, battering wind, my body pummelled on either side, each hit threatening to loosen my grasp and have me spiralling off into the void. I claw on, and soon see his shape. See him there, arms aloft, turning them around and working this tornado to the earth.

Only, no…it's not a *him* at all.

I see the long, flowing hair, and the curved shape of the hips. I see the silhouette of a woman, her power vast, and beyond a minor moment of surprise, feel nothing else at all.

In fact, it spurs me on to kill this bitch.

A fresh energy fills me, and with a last rush I reach her, crossing some odd threshold and entering into a world of total calm. About two metres all around her, there is no wind at all. It's quiet, still, the heart of the tornado a peaceful place in the middle of hell.

She looks at me, just seeing me crawl into her private domain from the corner of her eye. The shock is total, her eyes widening and lips parting.

"How…" I hear her whisper in the sudden calm, her face not old but not young either. Just a normal woman with extraordinary gifts.

Gifts I'm about to take from her.

I draw my knife and stand, and move straight towards her. She seems to realise her end has come. Her arms stay aloft, as if inviting my knife in, presenting the target that I will not miss.

I line her up and plunge the blade into her chest, cutting through into her heart.

"Need," I growl. "Desperation. The instinct to survive. That's how…"

A smile hovers onto her lips, and a sudden convulse brings a spit of blood dribbling over them. And as her eyes flicker and start to fade, her arms fall and the storm quickly subsides.

And into the mud she sinks.

CHAPTER THIRTY

I turn straight around as the woman dies, and the rain of dust and debris begins to fall. The smoke floats off, thinning, and the clearing becomes clearer than ever.

I can see it all now, the wreckage of the camp, tents destroyed and bodies burning. The sonic machine lies in a wreck, and the world goes silent and still. I blink soot from my eyes and see my brother, low on the ground, clamber uneasily to his feet. He looks around as I am, and sees that our work here is done.

I rush straight for him, but find my legs giving way. I tumble and splash into a pool of mixed mud and blood, and feel myself lifted to my feet as Zander rushes over. He hugs me hard, both of us breathing loudly, before letting me go and pulling the mud and bundled fabric from his ears.

I do exactly the same, and the sensation is glorious. It's quiet, quieter than it's ever been, quieter than the deepest of silences, even though the sounds of war in the city are still so clear. I smile wide and shake my head, and a laugh rumbles up through me.

"Do you hear that," I say.

Zander listens.

"What?"

"Nothing...no wailing, no shrieking."

His eyes widen.

"Hatcher. Colonel Hatcher...he must have disabled the other machine!"

We look together to the north, still far from the city, and though the sounds of war are still clear, there's nothing else to hear. The other machine, we know, would still be audible from this far away. Our Stalker ally must have got the job done.

"I bet you never thought you'd be so thankful to a Stalker," I laugh.

My brother shakes his head, grinning.

"Never," he says. "Though, Hatcher's a bit more than just a Stalker."

"Well, I guess we can thank our esteemed grandfather for his support. We wouldn't have been able to do this without his men..."

"No, I guess not," grumbles Zander. "We should probably get back to him I suppose."

As we prepare to set off, I hear movement over near the tents. I turn to look and so does my brother. On instinct, I lift my pistol and he lifts his pulse rifle, and we guide them straight at the source of the sound.

We step forward, gently and quietly, and from one of the wrecked tents, partially smouldering, see a figure crawl out. I prepare to fire immediately but Zander's hand comes down on the gun, pushing it away.

He shakes his head.

"Not yet," he says, and moves forward.

I follow behind, tentative, and scan the crawling figure. It's a man, dressed similarly to the woman I've just killed. His frame looks familiar, and for a second I tense up, stopping as Zander moves forward.

And then I recognise him. I remember who he is.

"Shoot him, Zander!" I shout immediately.

My brother turns to me, confused.

I lift my pistol and aim it at the man's head, set to the pull the trigger. But as my arm swings into position, I feel my body suddenly lift from the earth, one of the strangest sensations of my young life. My feet rise off the ground, and I feel my limbs suddenly stuck in place, paralysed.

I look at my brother, whose eyes have gone stark, and call out into his head.

The Elemental! It's the Elemental who destroyed the wall!

He doesn't need to be told. He knows full well already. With me still held in mid-air, Zander doesn't swing his weapon as I did. He doesn't stand his ground and try to kill the man, who's now clambering to his feet, and lifting a hand in Zander's direction.

No, my brother is too smart for that. In a split second, he disappears, dashing off out of range of the Elemental. I watch him speed away, and then feel myself tossed off to the side, crashing into the earth ten metres away. I land with such force that my mind goes muddy, and my eyes flicker, blurring as I watch the injured Elemental climb gingerly to his feet.

I see the blood seeping from his leg, see him put his weight on one side of his body. It must have been as I thought. He must have come here to rest and regain his energy after destroying the wall. He must have been in the tent when we attacked, his leg injured by some stray bullet or shrapnel. But clearly, he's got some gas left in the tank.

He stands now, turning his eyes off to his left where Zander dashes, his frame leaving a trail of clear air amid the mist. Then he looks back at me, and raises a hand, and I feel my body fix again where it is.

Dragging his limp leg, he approaches me, eyes glancing around the devastated camp and narrowing in anger. His lips form into a snarl, and I begin to feel the tremors in the earth, the muddy patch in which I lie starting to boil and froth.

"Looks like your friend has abandoned you," he growls. "Smart boy. You're not going to be so lucky."

The ground continues to bubble, then starts to split. It breaks apart, and I feel my paralysed frame begin to sink into the filth, the fingers of the earth creeping around me, dragging me into the depths.

"The earth is calling you, girl. Take a final breath now. It will be your last."

His fingers twist and coil, and the earth moves with them. Layers of mud and grime begin to wrap me up, covering every inch of me except for my face. He continues to slip forward, hauling his body along wearily, wanting to get as close as possible to see the terror in my eyes.

And fearful they are. I have mere moments left until I'm completely consumed. Moments that, while terrifying, I know won't be my last.

Because in my head, I hear him. He speaks to me, comforts me, guides me.

It's OK, Brie. I'm here, he says. *Keep him talking. Keep him distracted. I'll be back with you momentarily.*

The dirt and filth continues to gather. It licks at my skin, creeping closer around the edges of my face, my body now entirely devoured and locked tight in the earth. But my eyes are still uncovered, and my nose and mouth too. And before they go under, I whisper through my lips.

"You're not going to win," I say. "We have taken away your tricks. Our soldiers will overcome yours now, and you know it, don't you?"

I manage a smirk of my own, and see his eyes flash red.

"No...oh no, girl, you are mistaken," he growls. "Either way, you'll never find out."

His evil grin returns, and the mud creeps towards my nostrils and up my nose. I try to blow it out but it just keeps coming. The Elemental's smile doesn't leave him. He doesn't turn his eyes away. He watches, leaning closer, as his mind pulls the dirt and grime in whichever direction he wishes, filling my nostrils and then clearing them out, teasing the corners of my mouth.

His sadism is his downfall. He is making a terrible mistake.

To believe Zander abandoned me here to save his own skin…well, he doesn't know Zander, and he doesn't know me. Perhaps, in his world, such selfishness and cowardice is the norm.

Not here.

And as his smirk intensifies, I carve my own mouth into a look of calm as I hear my brother's voice once more.

It whispers quietly, comfortingly. I take a breath and my airways are covered.

I'm here, my brother says.

And as he says it, and the mud closes in, I see him appear as if from nowhere. Suddenly, he's there, right behind the Elemental, his form taller and prouder, face handsome and young. His eyes glow bright, and in a moment of terrible realisation, I witness the flow of panic rumble across my torturers face.

His mind may be powerful, but it isn't quick enough to hold my brother back. Before he even knows he's there, the knife is slipping across his throat, and the pain and fear is bubbling up through him. The gush of blood that comes next is a sight for sore eyes, and with only my eyes left uncovered, I see it all come frothing and spraying like a fountain from his opened throat.

But Zander isn't quite done. To complete the man's ignominious death, he grabs him with both arms, summons his own consummate gifts, and throws him with a great deal of pace and power towards a nearly tree trump. His aim is perfect, and the Elemental's body connects with a loud crack that tells of a splintered spine.

Back broken, and body paralysed, he can merely lie there with his body emptying of all its blood, and watch as Zander quickly digs me out of my grave. His arrogance and failure are as all consuming as each other. He has lost. And his army will now lose too.

Escaping the mire, I stand by my brother, drenched in filth and now wishing for the cool water of the pool not too far away. We watch the man's body give out, and smile in victory as he takes his final, gargled breath.

Two Elementals killed. The sonic machine destroyed.

All in all, not a bad night's work.

CHAPTER THIRTY ONE

We have no time to bask in our triumph here at the camp. I have little time, too, to thank my brother for saving my life. Again.

Such a thing has become the norm, yet my gratefulness remains profound. I hug him to show how much he means to me, how much I love him. Yet no words are required. Really, there are no words to express my thanks.

Turning our attention back to the little base here in the burnt out woods, we quickly check each enemy soldier to make sure they're dead. Once that's confirmed, we set off west, moving with as much speed as we can given the state of exhaustion that now grips us both with all available digits and limbs.

Already, the night is starting to head towards morning. With the smoke clearing, the shape of natural clouds in the sky above appear, and the silver lines of dawn become visible off on the distant horizon.

Moving through the brush, the sounds of war in the distance still rumble and chatter away, and without Zander's radio we can only hope that they're holding the lines and keeping the enemy from getting to the walls of Inner Haven.

I have some confidence now, a burgeoning feeling that we're gonna win this damn thing. Inner Haven is well protected, its walls similarly armed and bolstered and, given it's size relative to the perimeter of Outer Haven, far easier to defend. The strategy was always to hold the outer walls until, in the event that they fell, pull back gradually through the city, fighting from the many security cordons and blockades along the way.

The final stage is Inner Haven, and should it be needed, that's where the final stand will be made. Yet, with the smoke clearing and the wailing gone, our City Guards and other soldiers will find their many gifts returned. It will, hopefully, have evened things out, if not given us a distinct advantage.

After all, defending a city is far easier than trying to sack one. We have armaments and grand walls on our side, and far greater knowledge of the streets too. This fight is now ours for the taking. And right now, I want to get back to it as soon as possible.

So on we press, rushing through the brush without the need to stay silent. With our eyes now unencumbered by the fading mist, and the thick network of trees burnt away and no longer obscuring our view, we see everything ahead. Together, our Hawk eyes scan and search as we hurry on, just in case some enemy patrol should have heard the fighting and come to investigate.

The going is quick, however. Though we don't use our Dasher powers, we still jog as fast as we can manage, keen to return to Cromwell and work out just what to do next.

There are still many questions that need answering, and I'm sure, now that Zander knows the truth, we'll have plenty to discuss regarding just what we do with our old grandfather. Most likely, my brother's form of justice will be different from my own. Were it down to me, I'd execute the man as soon as we got a chance. Zander is more level-headed, though, and as his ire begins to sooth, and his logical manner of thinking returns, he might just choose to take a fairer path.

After all, without Cromwell's help, we would have had no chance over the last few days, and the days to come. Does that aid, this pact of ours, absolve him of former crimes? His crimes are certainly manifold, and go far beyond those against my family. My desire for revenge centres on my parents, but beyond them, all those who have died in this war have done so due to him. And though we've killed many innocents ourselves, we've done so purely as a reaction to his terrible doctrines that go against the basic rights all humans, both Enhanced and Unenhanced, should have.

That is all a discussion for another time, and Lady Orlando will no doubt have a very powerful voice within it. As far as I see it, if Zander and I want personal revenge, now might be the only time for it. We could enact our vengeance now, and pray that killing the man doesn't unleash his Stalkers and Con-Cops and turn them against us. So sneaky is he, so shrewd, that I truly don't know whether he's telling the truth on that count or not.

And, I suppose, that alone is enough to stay our hands right now. If we killed him, and returned to find our soldiers embroiled again in civil conflict, we'd never be able to forgive ourselves. Cromwell's death, though something I greatly desire, is far overshadowed by the risk his demise might bring.

No, we will continue to protect him, continue to save his life. In order to ensure the safety of our people, we have no choice in the matter.

We press forward, and the sight of the cliff nears, and the gentle sounds of the waterfall fills our ears. It's a lovely sound, and the anticipation of dowsing myself in the clear water and cleaning myself of this filth is enough to set a giddy feeling inside me.

Working through the marshes, and around the formations of rock, we gather our pace until, not far away, we spy the spout of water spewing from the cliffside. The lake then comes into view, and we conduct a very quick check, just before stepping towards it, to ensure that no one is around.

I see nothing, no movement at all. Satisfied, we continue our jog, working to the lake's shore and around it, feet squelching in the soft mud as we approach the western edge and head straight for the rocks and cave in which Cromwell lies.

As we go, I catch Zander stopping in my periphery. I stop too, a pace after him, and turn to find his eyes looking upon the muddy ground with a curious slant set upon his brow.

"What's up?" I ask casually.

He doesn't answer immediately. Then I see what he's looking at.

Prints. Footprints in the mud.

"They're ours, aren't they?" I ask, hopefully.

His eyes flick up, but not to me. They look straight at the rocks ahead, and he bursts forward and right past me. I barely have time to see what he's doing before he's clambering towards the cave and disappearing. I follow, running to catch up, working my way towards the little cavern…

I'm stopped by the reappearance of my brother, coming out the other way. His eyes are sharp and jaw clenched tight. I know immediately what's going on.

"He's gone, isn't he?" I ask.

He steps out and through the rocks, nodding and looking again at the tracks. They seem to be heading off to the west, disappearing into the scorched forest.

"Yes," he says. "Cromwell's gone. Or…he's been taken."

He turns to me, eyes gliding across my face and then in the direction of the city. Then they go the other way, back to the tracks. The intimation is clear.

"We're not heading back to the city yet, are we?" I ask.

He shakes his head, but doesn't speak.

And in my head, all I can think is that the attack on the camp was a little too easy. Or, that it went a little too well.

In my life, nothing is ever that easy. Nothing ever goes quite that well.

And the fates have played us again.

We have to go after our grandfather.

THE END

The Enhanced will conclude in Book Ten...

To hear about the author's latest discounts and new releases, sign up to his newsletter at www.tcedgebooks.com

Made in the USA
Columbia, SC
05 September 2021